This book belongs to:

. . . . . . . . . . . . . . . . . . . .

Praise for

MONSTER HUNTING for BEGINNERS

## Reviews from AUTHORS!

'A monstrously funny new voice!' Maz Evans,
author of *Who Let The Gods Out?*

'The best kind of children's book: funny, fast paced
and bursting with adventure. The brilliant pictures
match the story perfectly. You'll gobble this book up!'
Jenny McLachlan, author of *The Land of Roar*

'A magnificently hilarious masterpiece of monster
proportions. I howled with laughter!'
Jenny Pearson, author of *The Super Miraculous
Journey of Freddie Yates*

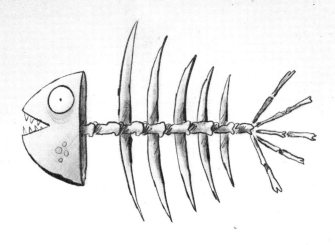

## Reviews from READERS!

'You could, if you were lazy, call this Pratchettesque.'

'Dazzlingly silly and brilliantly fun, *Monster Hunting for Beginners* is bulging and burping with vivid originality, side-splitting mayhem, and an impressive cast of eccentric creatures that quite frankly give the likes of *Monsters Inc* and *The Addams Family* a good run for their money.'

'This book is pure fun from start to finish and, as a parent, what more could you ask for?'

'I cannot recommend this book enough. It was an absolute pleasure to read, and my kids were so engaged with Jack's story that it's a book we will be reading over and over again.'

'This isn't Michael Morpurgo.'

First published in Great Britain 2023 by Farshore
An imprint of HarperCollins*Publishers*
1 London Bridge Street, London SE1 9GF

www.farshore.co.uk

HarperCollinsPublishers
Macken House, 39/40 Mayor Street Upper,
Dublin 1, D01 C9W8, Ireland

Text copyright © Ian Mark 2023
Illustrations copyright © Louis Ghibault 2023
The author and illustrator have asserted their moral rights.

ISBN 978 0 7555 0197 7

Printed and bound in the UK using 100% renewable electricity
at CPI Group (UK) Ltd

1

A CIP catalogue record for this title is available from the British Library.

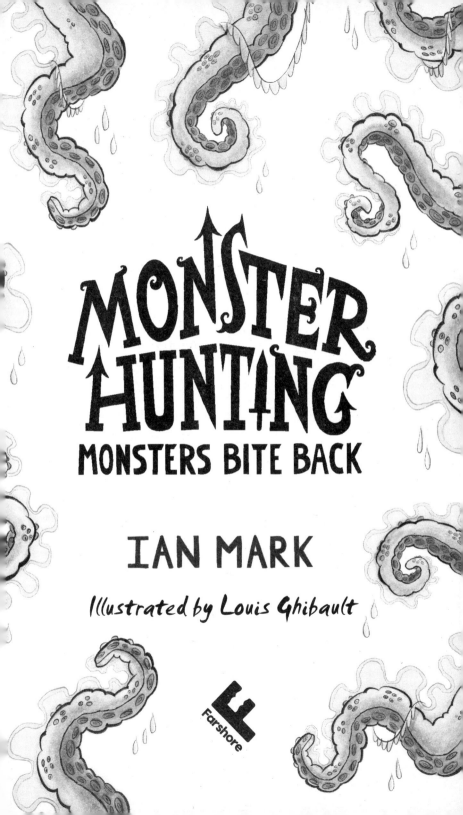

# MONSTER HUNTING
## MONSTERS BITE BACK

### IAN MARK

*Illustrated by Louis Ghibault*

Farshore

# Good Question

People often ask me: "Jack, what are the scariest monsters you've ever faced?"

They call me Jack because that's my name, and it would be silly to call me anything else.

They ask me about monsters because, well, I'm a monster hunter.

Don't laugh.

You don't have to be big or strong to fight monsters. If you did, I wouldn't be doing it. Monster hunters come in all shapes and sizes.

I found that out when a little man with a big beard called Stoop made me his apprentice, after I somehow . . . accidentally . . . I'm still not sure how . . . defeated an Ogre in single combat. It's all explained in my first adventure, and you should probably read that one before going any further to avoid confusion.

It's not entirely necessary. This story SHOULD make sense on its own, though I can't say for certain because I haven't finished writing it yet. In fact, I've only started.*

Since then, despite being smaller than most, and still only ten, I've squared up to many monsters, from Boggles and Bugbears and Boggy-Boes to Breaknecks and Kerfuffles and Bullbeggars and Brollachans and Boo-Hoos.**

And those are just the ones beginning with B. (Apart from the Kerfuffles. They must've slipped into the list when I wasn't looking.)

They're all to be found in the pages of a magical book called *Monster Hunting For Beginners*, which was given to me on my first day as an apprentice monster hunter.

Each time a new monster is discovered anywhere in the world, the monster hunter

* *You probably noticed that.*
**Boo-Hoos are so-called because they're always crying.*

2

who discovers it only has to write up the details in his or her copy of the book, and the new entry instantly appears in every other volume.

No matter how many monsters are added to it there's always room for more.

Here's what it says about Kerfuffles.

# Kerfuffle

*A kerfuffle means a fuss, and Kerfuffles are so called because that's what they like making. If yaks had been named for the same reason, they'd be called Big Piles of Poo. Of course, it's not the yaks' fault they have nowhere else to go but up a mountain, but that's no consolation when you've stepped into one of those piles in your new climbing boots.*

*Kerfuffles actually do look like yaks. Or what yaks would look like if they looked like giant porcupines. Their favourite activity is to curl up in a ball and roll over their enemies until they're so full of holes they spring a leak. The only way to defeat them is to put a little cork at the end of each of their sharp spines, but that takes ages.*

*It's much quicker and more effective to RUN AWAY when they're in the mood to make a fuss. (Which is always.) I'd do that if I were you.*

very sharp spikes

As you can tell, *Monster Hunting for Beginners* is not always helpful.
But which monsters are scariest?
That's easy.
It's these ones.

# Little Monsters

I don't blame you for being baffled.

Those are clearly not monsters.

They're children.

Children are not officially classed as monsters, but, take my word for it, they can be alarming under **Certain Circumstances**.

That's why they do have an entry of their own in *Monster Hunting for Beginners*.

# Children

*Children have many things in common with monsters. They're LOUD. They're unpredictable. They can also be VERY dangerous, especially when lots of them are gathered together. Monster hunters are advised to avoid areas where too many children are found and go instead to safer places, such as snake-infested jungles. Better safe than sorry.*

I felt like I'd looked at that page a hundred times already this morning, and each time the words on the cover had been different.

That was another of the book's magical qualities. The title constantly changed depending on who was holding it and how they were feeling at that moment.

Right now, it was called *Monster Hunting For Boys Who Wish They Could Disappear.*

The reason was, it was my first day at a new

school and I'd always been shy about meeting people. I'd rather face a monster any day!

I stood at the school gate, peering through the bars at all the children tearing round the yard, and my stomach started churning.

I wasn't just scared.

I wasn't just terrified.

I was **SCERRIFIED**.

"Don't worry," said Nancy.

Nancy is my best friend. She's also my only friend of my own age.*

I'd met her when I first came to King's Nooze. She'd helped me defeat a whole army of monsters led by Aunt Prudence.**

Now we saw each other every day and often headed off on adventures together.

"The kids here are no different from you and me," Nancy said as the minutes ticked down to the **Fateful Moment** when I'd have to step through the gate. "Well, they're a bit different from you and me, because they don't

* Stoop is my friend too, but he's 200 years old.
** She wasn't really my aunt, but that's another story. Literally.

fight monsters, but you know what I mean."

She squeezed my hand reassuringly.

Unfortunately, Nancy doesn't know her own strength, so it did make me scream a bit.

The sound was drowned out by the bell ringing to mark the start of the school day. I was about to embark on my **Most Terrifying Mission Ever**.

I took a deep breath . . . and walked in.

# School Daze

Nancy was right.* It wasn't too bad, even if the other children all looked at me as if I was a film they'd come to see, and they were wondering when it was going to start and if it would be worth watching to the end.

The teacher introduced me.

"Say hello to Jack, everyone," she said.

"Hello, Jack," everyone said back.

Miss Higgins asked me to say a few words so that the other children could get to know me.

I told them my mother was dead, and I'd moved here to King's Nooze with Dad.

---

* Nine times out ten she was, as she's asked me to point out.

I didn't say anything about my parents being monster hunters back in the day, or that I was one now too. In my old school, the kids had teased me for believing in monsters.

Thankfully, these kids didn't laugh at me. They were too busy laughing – in a good way – at Angela, who made the sound of a trombone every time she farted.

Which she did an Awful Lot.*

Miss Higgins didn't think it was funny, and kept saying "Angela, is that absolutely necessary?" and "I really think you should see a doctor, that doesn't sound at all healthy."

It was weird to think I'd saved everyone here from an invasion of Ogres just before the start of the summer holidays.

None of them remembered what had happened, because that's the way it is with monsters. Sometimes it's better to forget.

"I told you there was nothing to be scerrified about," said Nancy, as we sat eating

* If you don't know what a trombone sounds like, it's exactly the same as one of Angela's farts.

our sandwiches at lunchtime. "Nothing out of the ordinary ever happens in school."

She was wrong about that. It doesn't happen often,* which is why I remembered it.

---

* *Just one time out of ten, as I previously mentioned.*

# Not Now Arthur

It was the end of my first week at school, and we were all outside playing rounders.

I couldn't see the point of being good at games. Nobody ever died because they were bad at them. (Apart from that boy in the Isle of Wight last year, and everyone knows it was his own fault for playing tennis when he didn't have a ball.*)

We were sorted into teams and Miss Higgins tossed a coin to see who'd bat first.

Nancy's team won.

I was put out deep in the field.

That suited me fine. The ball hardly ever came this far. I could daydream about what

* He used a grenade instead.

monsters I might see next. There were still so many that I hadn't encountered . . .

The sound of a trombone announced the start of the game.

("Angela, will you stop that?")

After a while, I couldn't help noticing that there was a penguin with a letter in its beak, standing at the edge of the field, staring at me.

Very hard.

This might seem odd in England, even in Cornwall, which is where King's Nooze was.* But I was used to penguins.

The International League of Monster Hunters used carrier penguins to send out calls for help when there was a new monster which needed tackling. It wasn't the most efficient system in the world,

* And still is, last time I checked.

BANG!

because penguins
can't fly. And they can't
drive either, because it's hard
to hold on to the steering wheel
with flippers and their feet can't
reach the pedals.

"Not now, Arthur!" I hissed, because
I recognised the penguin at once. "You
know I can only hunt monsters outside
school hours."

Arthur went on staring.

Harder.

On the other side of the field, it was
Nancy's turn to bat.

She readied herself for the ball, then swung
back her arm, and clobbered it with all
her might.*

The ball soared in my direction.

I looked up, blinking in the sun.

"Catch it!" yelled Angela, adding an
extra loud parp for emphasis.

* The ball, that is, not her own arm.

14

I tried to concentrate, but Arthur was
waddling on to the field to deliver his letter.

The ball had almost reached me.

I opened my hands to catch it. I'd be the
hero. I'd have got a player out for my team.

Closer it came.

Closer.

At the last moment, the penguin made
a paper aeroplane out
of the letter and
tossed it in my
direction. I could see
it approaching at
an angle out of
the corner of
my eye.

The corner of my
eye was exactly
where it made
contact.

"Ouch!"

My hands flew to my face, and the ball bounced off the top of my head . . .

"Ouch, again!"

. . . then thudded to the ground, together with my glasses.

My teammates groaned with disappointment.

By the time I'd picked up my glasses and put them back on, Arthur was already off on his next mission.

I picked up the letter and stuffed it in my pocket, wondering what was so urgent that the International League of Monster Hunters would risk attracting **Undue Attention** by sending a penguin to my school.

# Eew Stew

"You didn't have to hit it so hard," I said to Nancy as we walked home after school.

"Sorry," she said. "I meant to go easy on you, but I couldn't resist. I saw the ball coming towards me and had an **Uncontrollable Urge** to whack it." She mimicked the action. "Did you hear everyone cheering?"

"No, I was too busy picking a paper aeroplane out of my eye," I reminded her. "Didn't anyone notice the penguin?"

"They thought it was a dog."

"Dogs don't have wings."

"Some do," she pointed out.* "But never mind that. I want to see what the letter says."

* She was probably thinking of the famous Flying Poodles of Panama. Trust me, you don't want to be standing underneath one of those when it has an upset tummy.

Eagerly, I tore open the envelope and took out the message. Here's what it said.

Lubbers here! Lubbers there! There are Lubbers everywhere! Come quickly, Jack, and get rid of them – or it will be too late, and too late is the worst time to deal with anything, especially Lubbers.
Yours fearfully,
The Sisters of Perpetual Misery

"Perpetual means never-ending," said Nancy helpfully.

"I know!" I said.*

"Those Lubbers sound serious," she went on with a thrill in her voice at the prospect of a new adventure. "Where do these fearful,

* I didn't.

18

never-endingly miserable Sisters live?"

I turned over the letter, and there on the back was an address.

Muckle Abbey,
Muckle,
Quite Near The Top Of Scotland,
Great Britain,
Planet Earth,
The Solar System,
The Milky Way,
Outer Space,
The Universe, Etc.
(Sorry, we're not sure what comes
after The Universe.)

"Come on, Nancy," I said. "We'd better pick up Stoop and get on our way at once."

Together we raced to the little house on the edge of King's Nooze where Dad and I now lived, dumped our school bags in the hall and burst into the kitchen at a gallop.

**Oh no**.

Dad was wearing an apron.

That could only mean One Thing.

He was cooking.

To say that Dad wasn't a very good cook was the **Understatement Of All Time**. He didn't cook food so much as burn it beyond recognition. The moment I walked into the kitchen, my nose started to shudder as if it was trying to detach itself from my face and run away in horror from the awful stink.

"Jack, Nancy, what do you think?" Dad said cheerfully, reaching for a spoon so that we could sample the black and oozy stew he had bubbling on the stove.

"Dad, we don't have ti–"

He slipped a spoon between my lips before

I could finish what I was going to say.

"Delicious!" I lied, trying not to gag.*

"Some for you, Nancy?" suggested Dad.

"I'd love to," Nancy said.** "But we need to speak to Stoop, fast! Where is he?"

"In the potting shed as usual," said Dad. "That reminds me. I must add some extra ingredients to the stew especially for him. You know how much he loves cabbage."

"Yum," I said with a feeling of dread, making for the back garden before Dad could invite me to taste another shocking spoonful.

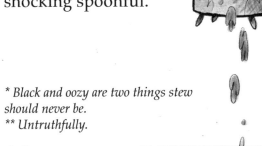

* Black and oozy are two things stew should never be.
** Untruthfully.

# Fleasy Peasy

The potting shed was at the bottom of the garden, where potting sheds usually are.

The previous owners of the house, being normal people, had used it to store their trowels and rakes and bottles of weed killer.

Stoop had immediately thrown them out and moved in.

"You can have one of the extra bedrooms upstairs," we'd offered, but he refused. He said a monster hunter's job was not to **Wallow In Luxury**, but to be ever ready for adventure,

and you couldn't do that in a comfy bed.*

I knocked on the door.

"Go away!" bellowed a familiar voice.

He always said that. He didn't mean it. I opened the door and stepped inside.

Stoop was sitting cross-legged on the shed floor, warming his hands at the fire which he kept constantly burning in an old saucepan because he hated the cold.

He was dressed, as always, in a leather tunic and tin helmet. I'd never seen him wear

---

*I disagree. My bed is very soft and it gives me something to look forward to when I come home after a hard day's monster hunting.

anything else, except once – but only once –
when he sent his monster hunting outfit to be
cleaned and spent the day in pyjamas.

"There you are," he said grumpily.* "Where
have you been all week?"

"In school," I said.

"You had to stay there for the **WHOLE**
week?" said Stoop in disbelief.

"Yes, that's how it works. I also have to go
back next week."

"WHAT?"

"And the one after that. And the one after
that. We've been through this a million times."

"School, school, school!" said Stoop, shaking
his head. "What's the use? I left when I was
five. I only went there for one day before
deciding it wasn't for me."

"Don't blame us," said Nancy. "We're not
exactly dancing a jig about it either."

Stoop wasn't listening.

"What's up with your eye?" he said to me.

"Arthur threw a letter at me," I explained,

* *That's how he said everything.*

glad of the chance to get back to the business at hand. "Here. Take a look at it."

"Why would I want to look at your eye? I've seen it loads of times. It's right there on your face next to the other one."

"I meant look at the letter."

"You should have said so then."

Getting to his feet, Stoop grabbed the piece of paper and held it up to his nose to read. It didn't take long. There were only forty-two words in the entire message, if you cut out the very long, silly address.*

Only when he turned the message over to that very address did his eyes widen for a second, as if in alarm, before he controlled himself and handed it back with a scoff.

"Sisters of Perpetual Misery indeed," he snorted. "Never heard of them! Trust me, this is someone's idea of a joke. And it's not a funny one either, like the one about what kind of dog a magician has.** Lubbers aren't even dangerous. Look them up and you'll see."

* That's the same number of words as in this paragraph.
** The answer is a Labracadabrador.

I checked in my *Monster Hunting* book under L for Lubbers.

# Lubbers

monk
hairdo

little
horns

little
hooves

small
tail

a habit

These are Lubbers. Don't look very scary, do they?
That's because they're not. But they do make quite
a menace of themselves in old abbeys by swarming
out at night and raiding the larder.
They look like monks, but with little hooves and
pointy ears. Their presence makes itself known by

*hoofprints in the butter. That's better than finding elephant prints in the butter, which, as everyone knows, is how you know if there's an elephant hiding in your fridge.*

*The other way of spotting them is if you happen to notice a large swarm of small, monk-like creatures with little hoofs and pointy ears running round your old abbey in the middle of the night. That's what we in the trade call a Dead Giveaway.*

Admittedly, it didn't sound very urgent.

"Of course it's not," said Stoop. "There used to be Lubbers living nearby when I was a nipper. They had some wild parties all right. The neighbours had to pop round many nights to ask them to turn down the music and stop singing rude songs. But they never did any Real Harm. Lubbers are merely a nuisance. Like fleas. You wouldn't call in a monster hunter if your dog had fleas, would you?"

"I suppose not," I said.

"You suppose right. You'd go to the vet and buy some flea powder. Whoever sent you this nonsensical message should just put down traps and release the Lubbers back into the wild. That's what everyone else does. It's easy. Easy peasy. Fleasy peasy, you might say."

He chuckled at his joke.

"That's not the point," I said firmly. "They asked for my help. We can't ignore it."

"I can," said Stoop, sitting back down and folding his arms stubbornly. "Just watch me ignoring it. Do you see me ignoring it? I'm ignoring it right now. I've never ignored anything more than I'm ignoring this. I could go on ignoring it all night."

I turned to Nancy for help, but she was staring at the letter again.

"You can't ignore it, Stoop," she said quietly. "I've just noticed another section at the bottom of the letter. It must have been written in invisible ink and the heat from the fire made it appear. It speaks of an ancient prophecy which states . . ." – she squinted at the page – "if the Sisters of Perpetual Misery are ever forced to leave Muckle Abbey, it will bring about THE END OF THE WORLD AS WE KNOW IT!"

# Hunters can't be Choosers

"Does it really say that?" I said in amazement.

"Of course it doesn't," protested Stoop irritably. "How could a few Lubbers bring about the end of the world as we know it?"

"You're saying it wrong," said Nancy. "It's **THE END OF THE WORLD AS WE KNOW IT.**"

"I don't give a fig. You're making it up."

"I am not! It's right here in black and white," she declared, jabbing a finger at the bottom of the page. "See for yourself."

Nancy held out the message for Stoop to read, but at the last moment she let it go and it dropped into the fire and was frazzled up like bacon left in the frying pan too long.*

---

* That's what happened to most of our bacon, thanks to Dad.

Stoop tried grabbing the last pieces before it burned away completely, but he only managed to singe his fingers.

"Oops," said Nancy.

"You did that deliberately!" said Stoop.

"No, I didn't. Anyway, this changes everything. If there's even a slight chance that the world might end if we do **NOTHING**, then we must do **SOMETHING**."

She was right. Again. It was written in the monster hunting Code of Honour.

*A monster hunter's main job is to protect people from all monster-related dangers. That's not easy because people are always putting themselves stupidly into peril, but if you don't like it then you should have got yourself a nice, safe, easy job such as being a trapeze artist or Bigfoot wrestler or someone who mixes Nuclear Milkshakes instead.*

Stoop knew when he was beaten.

No self-respecting monster hunter would let his own feelings get in the way of answering a Desperate Cry For Help.

"HELP!"

Yes, a desperate cry for help like that.

Wait, that was Dad's voice. There wasn't a moment to lose, and I didn't lose it.

I darted back to the house, ready to do what was necessary to save him.

# Goo and Goodbye

Dashing into the kitchen, I saw Dad struggling violently with the pot of stew. It was gurgling crazily on the stove as if it was about to blow.

Then it did.

With an enormous thunderclap, the lid flew off and stew spurted everywhere, covering the walls of the kitchen in black goo.

"There must have been something wrong with the cabbage," Dad sighed.

"A bad cook always blames his cabbage," said Stoop, stepping into the kitchen a moment later. "Don't worry, we'll get a bite to eat when we reach our destination."

"Where are you going?" asked Dad, doing his best not to show how anxious he felt whenever I went off on a new mission.

"We're going to Scotland to tackle an outbreak of Lubbers," I said.

"But Lubbers aren't dangerous," he replied. "They're more like –"

"Fleas, I know! Stoop already told me. But I have to go. The Sisters of Pertep . . . Perpep . . . Never-Ending Misery need our help."

"You know best, Jack," said Dad.

Quickly, I ran to my room and changed into my special monster hunting outfit in preparation for another adventure.

Tin helmet . . . leather tunic . . . belt.

Last of all, my seven league boots. They were the best things I'd been given since becoming a monster hunter – apart from *Monster Hunting for Beginners*, of course.

They were called seven league boots because that's how far you could travel with each step when wearing them. (A league is an old fashioned way of saying three miles, so they should really be called twenty-one mile boots to be more modern.*)

Nancy didn't have her own pair of seven league boots, because she wasn't officially a monster hunter yet. She didn't think that was fair and I didn't either, but Stoop said rules were there for a reason, even if he could never remember what the reason was in this case.

Whenever we went monster hunting, Nancy borrowed Dad's old seven league boots instead. They were far too big for her feet so she had to wear at least four pairs of the woolliest socks to make them fit, and they were also a bit slow on account of their age.

In fact, they were now more like three and a half league – or ten and a half mile – boots.** But they did the job, and that's what mattered.

"All set?" I said, slipping *Monster Hunting for Beginners* into my bag.

"Ready when you are."

"Then let's go!"

* Or 33.796224 kilometre boots, though that's not as snappy.
** Or 16.89811 kilometre boots, if you insist.

# Boy Meets Wall

The first time I tried walking in seven league boots, I ended upside down in a tree.

I had the hang of them now, and could get about in a pair as easily as if I was walking to the shops for a sausage roll.

In one step, we were out of King's Nooze.

In five, we'd left Cornwall behind, and were skipping from county to county as if we were crossing a river on stepping stones.

I always took great pleasure in the astonished looks on people's faces when they saw us passing overhead at speed.

They didn't know they were seeing three monster hunters on their way to a new assignment. They didn't know **WHAT** they were seeing. The trickiest bit was avoiding low-flying planes, because the last thing people want to see when they're high up in the air in a metal tube going on holiday is someone whizzing past the window at top speed. And I could only imagine that seeing three someones is even **MORE** alarming.

Soon the whole of England had unfurled below us, and the Scottish border came into sight.

That was odd. Borders are usually invisible. They're just lines on a map that mark where one country ends and another begins.

This border wasn't like that today.

It was more like . . . a wall? A solid, shimmering, silver-grey wall.

I didn't like the look of it at all, but it was too late to slow down.*

"Watch out!" yelled Nancy as she wheeled away. "You're going too fast!"

* It seemed I didn't have the hang of seven league boots as much as I thought.

I tried to put on the brakes, but seven league boots don't have any.
I slammed into the wall at full speed.

# Haven't the Foggiest

It hurt a lot less than I was expecting.

Come to think of it, it didn't hurt at all.

I sank into **The Wall That Wasn't A Wall** as if sinking into a great bowl of porridge.*

It smelled a bit like porridge too, but it wasn't. Porridge doesn't hang in the air like fog. That's what fog does, and fog is what this was. The cold tendrils grabbed hold of me and slowed me down until I stopped moving altogether, but I didn't fall. The fog was so thick that I was suspended in mid air.

"Stoop! Nancy! Where are you?" I called, unable to see either of them.

"I'm over here," came a single, distant, faint

*That did happen to me once, but I'm too busy right now to go into details, as the people who carried on reading the story, rather than getting distracted by this footnote, have already discovered.

reply from Stoop.

"That's not much help," I said, because I couldn't tell whether his voice was coming from left or right or up or down.

"Stay where you are and I'll wade over to you. I think I can make you out in the gloom . . . oh wait, that's not you. It's a passing albatross. I do apologise, madam."

Suddenly I heard Stoop gasp.

"Stay where you are and don't make any sudden movements," he ordered, and I could tell that **Something Was Wrong**.

"What's the matter? It's just fog, isn't it?"

"No, it's not. We've been caught in a crowd of Fog Goblins," said Stoop.

"What are they?"

"How many times do I have to tell you?" Stoop exclaimed. "If you want to know something about monsters, look in the book."

I reached into my bag for *Monster Hunting for Beginners*, and settled back on a squishy – if slightly clammy – lump of fog to read.

Unfortunately, I couldn't see a thing
because the fog had fogged up my glasses.

Here's what it would've said if I'd
seen it.

# Fog Goblins

use big fan to increase visibility

staff with spikes

pig noses

large ears

fog coming from skin

*If you ask them, teachers will tell you that fog is
made of compressed air. This is another reason
why you should never trust a word grown-ups say,
because they're shocking liars. To be fair, most fog
IS made that way, but now and again it's caused*

*by Fog Goblins. The fog comes off their skin like steam from a melting ice cube and makes them very hard to see. They can be dispersed with the use of a very big fan or, better still, a wind machine. Just blow it in their general direction. If caught in a patch of fog, do not make any sudden movements as Fog Goblins are notoriously mischievous.*

I was putting the book back in my bag, wondering what I was supposed to do now, when a huge hue and cry arose in the distance.

"Stoop, is that you?"

"**JaaaaaaaaaaAAAAAAaaaaaaaaaack**!" he yelled, suddenly accelerating towards me through the gloom at great speed, before shooting past, his voice fading into the distance, like a car passing on the road.

"Where are you?" I shouted again.

There was no answer.

Scared suddenly, I drew my sword.

# Who's For Hoo-Shank?

Two things should be pointed out at this stage. The first thing is that it wasn't really a sword.

Apprentice monster hunters are not allowed sharp weapons in case they hurt themselves – or, more importantly, as Stoop had made clear to me on many occasions, in case they hurt the monster hunter to whom they're apprenticed.

This was a wooden sword I'd made at home in the hope it would fool monsters into thinking that I was fearsome.

The most damage it had ever done was to ME when I got a splinter in my bum after sitting on it.

The second thing I should point out is that, even if I had owned a real sword, I wouldn't be allowed to use it against monsters anyway.

One of the most important rules of monster hunting is that we're not allowed to kill or injure the monsters we're sent to deal with. We have to catch and rehabilitate them instead.

That rule makes our job very hard sometimes, but monsters have feelings too.

I only drew my wooden sword now to show the Fog Goblins **I was Not To Be Messed With**. Unfortunately, you should NEVER draw your weapon in the presence of Fog Goblins, as I would have learned had I managed to read the rest of the entry on them in my book.

*You should NEVER draw your weapon in the presence of Fog Goblins. They're generally harmless, and will disperse of their own free will given time, but the sight of pointy things instantly puts them in a state of Heightened Alert, and they'll respond by doing what they always do when provoked, and that's play Hoo Shank.*

*What, you might ask, is Hoo Shank?*

*I'm glad you asked me that. Hoo Shank is the Fog Goblins' favourite game, the rules of which are too complicated to explain. Even the Fog Goblins don't really know how to play Hoo Shank, but they have so much fun playing it that they don't care if it makes no sense.*

Unluckily for me, I didn't get a chance to read that bit until later either.

As predicted, the Fog Goblins didn't take kindly to the sight of my sword.

"You're in for it now," shrieked a high-pitched voice gleefully.

Apparently, this was the moment they'd been waiting for. I felt myself being grabbed from behind by unseen foggy hands. The next moment . . .

. . . I was flung with **Great Force** through the fog until I was caught by a different Fog Goblin, and sent in a totally new direction, while they gibbered merrily.

This was Hoo Shank.

"Five nil!" came a triumphant shriek.

"Nil two!"

"Thirty!"

Back and forth I was thrown repeatedly, sometimes passing Stoop as he whizzed in the other direction.* I tried to grab hold of him to slow us both down, but it was useless.

I had no idea what had happened to Nancy. I only hoped that she'd avoided being swallowed by the oaty fog too.

"Nine-Wednesday!"

"Minus six!"

"In!"

"Out!"

"Shake it all about!"

---

*Clearly he had made the mistake of drawing his sword too.

The rules and scoring of this ridiculous game really did make no sense at all.

Soon I was so fed up of being flung to and fro that I would've swiped the Fog Goblins with my sword if I'd managed to stay still long enough. Who – or what – would I have used it on, though? I couldn't make out any figures, only glimpses of faces in the fog – weird distorted grins – shrill, high giggling – fog puffing from pig-like nostrils.

How long the game went on I couldn't say, because I never got a chance to check the time.* But eventually through the thick fog I heard the muffled sound of bells.

For some reason, every time the bells rang the fog became thinner and thinner, making the Fog Goblins shriek in annoyance.

Within seconds, the fog was no longer able to support my weight, and I found myself drifting like a leaf falling off a tree in autumn, down

*And I didn't have a watch anyway.

and down, until I lay on soft ground looking up as the sky cleared above me.

Sure at last that the Fog Goblins had dispersed, I stood up to see where I was.

# Cold Soup

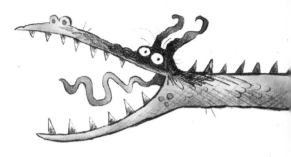

There in front of me was a large stretch of grey water surrounded on all sides by high mountains decked with purple heather.

It looked like a huge bowl of soup.

Very cold soup, with mist* curling off the water instead of steam.

Peering closely at the water, I thought I saw something flicker out there . . . the end of a tail, maybe? It lasted for the tiniest moment, then vanished with a plash.

It may even have been a splash, which is slightly bigger than a plash, but it certainly wasn't as big as a sploosh.**

"Did you see that?" I said uneasily.

"See what?" said Stoop, who'd also returned to earth and was inspecting each of his limbs in turn to make sure that they were attached to

---

* Real mist, not Mist Goblins, because there are no such things.
** It definitely wasn't a kersploosh, because they're ENORMOUS..

his body in the **Customary Way**.

I told him about the tail.

"It's probably the Loch Less Monster," he said with a shrug.

"Don't you mean the Loch Ness Monster?" I said, because I'd heard of her.

"If that's what I meant, I'd have said so," Stoop replied tetchily. He pointed at the soupy water. "That is Loch Less. It's like Loch Ness, only not as big. Hence the name. And like Loch Ness, this loch has a monster of its own, only she's much smaller than her more famous relative. She's known in these parts as Lessie."

"Is she fierce?"

"Not in the slightest, but someone wants us to think she is. Look!"

Every few yards along the shore, posts had been driven into the ground, with signs nailed on warning **MONSTER AT WORK** and **NOSEY PARKERS BEWARE!** and **TRESPASSERS WILL BE EATEN**.

"Lessie wouldn't eat anyone," said Stoop indignantly. "She's a vegetarian. Take it from me. I added her entry to *Monster Hunting for Beginners*. It was the first one I ever wrote. Have a peep inside and you'll see."

I reminded him we had more pressing problems at that moment than what some monstrous dweller in the loch ate for dinner.

"Like what?" he said.

"Like finding Nancy, for one thing."

Stoop said not to panic. The Fog Goblins had tossed us the entire length of Scotland, meaning we'd reached our intended destination **Quite Near The Top**. Nancy was bound to find her own way here soon enough.

"Why don't we ask if they've seen her at that house?" I said, pointing to a large building on a nearby headland overlooking Loch Less.

"That's no house," said Stoop, squinting at it as if he couldn't believe what he was seeing. "It's an abbey. So that's Muckle Abbey, is it?

Weird. Let's go. Last one there's a bampot."

I set off after him, staring up at Maybe-Muckle Abbey as it – or rather we – came nearer. It was hard to believe that anyone could live in such a grim and forbidding place.

No lights shone from any of the windows. No sound was coming from inside.

There wasn't even a doorbell.

I had to bang on the iron-barred front door as hard as I could with my fist.

No reply.

I knocked again.

I was about to knock a third time, because that's what always comes after the second time, unless you skip the third knock and go straight to the fourth – and that's just asking for trouble –

when a grille in the middle
of the door was pulled
back with a snap.

Two eyes peered out.

"Is this Muckle Abbey?"
I said.

"Who wants to know?"
said the eyes.

Or rather, it
wasn't the eyes who
said it, because
eyes
can't talk.

"I'm Jack," I said,
flashing a friendly
grin.

"Good for you,"
said the mouth of
the woman whose
eyes they were.
Then she slammed
the grille shut.

# And then there Were Nuns

I was so cross that I skipped the third and fourth knocks entirely, and went straight to the fifth. That would show them!

The grille opened immediately, and the same eyes glared out.*

"What do you want this time?"

"I told you. I'm Jack" – I waited for the grille to be slammed shut again, but it wasn't – "and this is Stoop. We got your message about the Lubbers and came at once to help."

"Well, why didn't you say so?"

"I did try," I said.

From inside came an excited murmur.

"It's them!"

* At least I assumed they were the same ones, though eyes all look alike really.

"They came!"

"I told you they would!"

"You did nothing of the sort, you fibber!"

"Did so!"

"Did not!"

"Right, you asked for it. Take that!"

"Get your hands off me!"

"Stop scrapping, you two!"

"Let Jack in, for goodness sake!"

"Who wants to play hopscotch?"*

Iron bolts were drawn back, and the door opened with a slow creak, though that was just Stoop adding his own sound effects to make the moment more atmospheric.

Together we stepped into a stone hall, lit with flaming candles on all sides.

In front of us stood a small group of nuns.

"Welcome to Muckle Abbey," said the nearest nun, stepping forward to greet us with a smile that stretched her rosy cheeks. "I am the head of the Sisters of Perpetual Misery.

* I'm not sure the last speaker was paying attention to what was going on.

My name is Nun The Wiser, and this is my assistant, Second To Nun."

A smaller nun, her face every bit as friendly, stepped forward and bowed her head.

"You have no idea how excited we are that you came in answer to our plea for help, Jack," said Nun The Wiser. "We've heard so much about your exploits. You're the very monster hunter we need! But what am I thinking? You haven't even met us all. Sisters, step forward and introduce yourselves."

 # Nun
by
Nun

It was difficult to tell the other nuns apart because they were all dressed alike in black robes, except for one who was dressed as a traffic warden for no apparent reason.

"Go and put on your proper costume," said Nun The Wiser sternly. "You've been warned about this before." The one who was dressed incorrectly scuttled off to change.

The other Sisters of Perpetual Misery took it in turns to tell us their names.

There was Nun At All and Nun Other. Nun Too Soon and Nun Left.

Nun Whatsoever came next, followed by Nun Of This and Nun Of That, and Nun Too Pleased who declared cheerily that this was the happiest day of her life.

Nun Of Your Business – who, Nun The Wiser explained, had turned up at Muckle Abbey one day and moved in, and still wouldn't tell anyone what she was doing there – merely nodded her head sharply in greeting, and refused to say another word.

Then it was the turn of Nun Of The Above, who was so named, she explained, because she lived in the highest room in Muckle Abbey.

Last of all came the smallest of the nuns.

Her name was Nun The Less, and she was very shy. She had to be prompted a number of times to step forward and say her name.*

"You must forgive us for not answering the door sooner," said Nun The Wiser. "We heard the Fog Goblins earlier and were afraid they'd sneak in again if we **Let Down Our Guard**."

"You've had trouble with them before then?" I said.

"They stole in one night a couple of weeks

---

* I remembered my first day at King's Nooze school and understood how she felt.

ago when someone carelessly left a window open, and spent a whole hour tossing Nun Of This back and forth. Or it may have been Nun Of That. I've never been able to tell them apart. Whichever it was, she was dizzy for a week."

"That was a good idea to ring the bells to disperse them," said Stoop. "Most monsters are upset by the sound of clanging."

"But that wasn't us," said Nun The Wiser. "We were sitting down to supper when they started pealing.* We were quite cross about it. It's steak and kidney pie tonight."

"If you didn't ring them," I said, "who did?"

"That," piped up a familiar voice from the back of the hall, "would be me."

---

* *That's another word for the sound bells make when rung.*

# Rules
## are
# Rules

"Nancy!" I said with relief, as our fellow monster hunter stepped from the shadows. "You got away from the Fog Goblins too."

"I didn't need to," said Nancy. "They were very sweet. When they heard that I was lost, they gladly brought me here themselves."

"Fog Goblins are not sweet!" said Stoop. "They're about as sweet as unripe, gherkin-flavoured gooseberries. They played Hoo Shank with us. I still have the bruises."

"You must have drawn your weapons," said Nancy, and I was forced to admit that I had.* "You don't need your own copy of *Monster Hunting for Beginners* to know that's the **Very Last Thing To Do** when dealing with Fog Goblins. Thankfully, I happen to know they

* *Stoop never admitted to anything if he could avoid it.*

CLANNGGG

hate the sound of
bells, so, when they
dropped me off,
I ran into the tower to ring them."

"I don't know what would've
become of us if you hadn't," I said
gratefully, but Stoop wasn't in the
mood to be generous.

The mention of steak and kidney
pudding had set his tummy rumbling
longingly.

He demanded to be taken AT ONCE
to the Lubbers so that we could put
down some traps and then concentrate
on more pressing matters, such as
getting something to eat.

"Alas, I'm afraid that won't be
possible," said Nun The Wiser
apologetically. "The Lubbers never
come out before midnight."

"Midnight's hours away," said Stoop. "I can't wait that long without a bite to eat."

"We'd love to offer you some food," said Nun The Wiser regretfully, "but it is strictly prohibited for us to eat with those who aren't members of our order. It's one of the **Three Golden Rules** of Muckle Abbey."

"What are the other two?" I said.

"The Second Rule is: No fizzy drinks before bedtime."

"That's sensible," I said, because I'd had a few accidents caused by that when younger, and there's nothing worse than sleeping on a soggy mattress. "What's the third?"

"The third and most important rule is never to tell anyone what the Third Rule is," Nun The Wiser said solemnly.

Nancy frowned. "That makes no sense. If that IS the Third Rule, then you've just told us what it is, thereby breaking the rule. Unless you're telling fibs, and I'm fairly sure that nuns aren't allowed to lie."

"You're right. Fibbing is forbidden," said Nun The Less. "That's the Fourth Rule."

"You said there were only Three Golden Rules," Nancy pointed out.

"So I did. The Fourth Rule is silver."

"Is there a Fifth Rule?" I wondered, with a funny feeling that I'd regret asking.

"The Fifth Rule," said Nun The Wiser, "is that the Sisters of Perpetual Misery must never leave Muckle Abbey. Surely you've heard of the ancient prophecy which warns that, if we ever do move out, the abbey will fall down and bring about . . ." – Nun The Wiser left a dramatic pause – "**THE END OF THE WORLD AS WE KNOW IT!**"

"But I thought I made that up," exclaimed Nancy, before clamping her hand over her mouth as she realised her mistake.

# The Pits

"I knew it," said Stoop, glowering at Nancy. "You tricked me into coming here."

"I'm sorry, Stoop," said Nancy. "It was the only way to convince you. I didn't know there really was a prophecy."

"Indeed there is," said Nun The Wiser. "It's written that this very abbey sits on an opening into the **Fiery Pits of Doom**. Also known as the **Underworld** for short."

"**The Underworld**?" I said with a quiver.

There was a section about **That Place** at the back of *Monster Hunting for Beginners*, but I still hadn't rustled up the courage to read it. I'd always hoped that I wouldn't need to.

The pages were slightly scorched and hot to

the touch and they came with a warning.

*Read on at your own peril!*

"Should we ever be forced to leave here," Nun the Wiser continued, "the prophecy says that Muckle Abbey will sink to its knees and the monsters who live down in the **Underworld** will be free to crawl out and wreak untold mischief and mayhem on the world."

"That's why we need you to deal with the Lubbers," said Second To Nun. "They're making such a nuisance of themselves that we feel we have no alternative but to leave anyway, even if it does cause the world to end. They run around all night, making a racket and pulling the sheets off our beds and leaving muddy hoofprints everywhere. And you should hear the shocking songs they sing. They're not suitable for our nunnish ears. We haven't had a wink of sleep in weeks."

"Very inconvenient, I'm sure," said Stoop, "but **THE END OF THE WORLD AS WE KNOW IT** won't be much fun either, so why not just stay and put up with them?"

"All things considered," said Nun The Wiser, "it really does sound as if we should."

"So are you going to?"

"No!" the nuns all cried together.

That settled it. Our mission was more urgent than ever. Standing there, I almost imagined that I could feel the heat from the **Underworld** rising up through the stone floor.

At least I hoped I was imagining it.

There was nothing for it but to return at midnight and deal with the Lubbers, thus keeping the **Fiery Pits of Doom** sealed forever.

In the meantime, Stoop insisted that we head to the nearest village and get something to

eat, because he couldn't be expected to stop **THE END OF THE WORLD AS WE KNOW IT** on an empty stomach.

"How do you know the way to the village anyway?" I said as the door of Muckle Abbey slammed tight behind us and Stoop set off along the bumpy, unlit road by the loch.

"Villages are generally in this direction," he said unconvincingly.

"Are they?"

"Stop asking questions!"

He refused to say another word until the village of Muckle came into sight, sitting on the edge of the loch as if it had stopped there after a long walk to bathe its feet in the water and decided to stay because it liked the view.

The little monster hunter definitely seemed to know where he was going.

He kept his head down and didn't look up once as he strode through the winding streets.

I saw people whispering as he passed.

Fingers pointed.

One man raised his hat to say hello, but Stoop grunted and ignored him.

"How do the villagers know who you are?" asked Nancy suspiciously.

"They must be mistaking me for someone else," he said as unconvincingly as before.

Nancy and I could see he wasn't ready to come clean, and decided to **Bide Our Time**.

We'd now reached the centre of the village.

There stood The Smuggler's Inn, though the name turned out to be a fib, because the smuggler wasn't in, she was out.

It was her brother who greeted us instead.

"Stoop," he said. "It's been too long."

# Feast is Feast

"Bring us food!" Stoop commanded.

The smuggler's brother must have been used to Stoop's gruffness.

"How will Sir be paying?" he said.

"Sir won't."

Stoop handed over a gold card with the words International League of Monster Hunters on the front.

The League footed the bill for all Reasonable Expenses when monster hunters were on official business, as well as entitling the holder to free cabbage from every market stall this side of Constantinople.*

---

* On the other side of Constantinople, you had to use a secret password which was changed weekly for security reasons.

We were led to a table next to a blazing fire, and soon the table was spread with a tempting assortment of nibbles, nosh and nourishment.*

There was Welsh rarebit, French toast, Irish stew, German sausage, Spanish omelette, Greek yoghurt, Turkish delight, Danish pastries, Scotch eggs and English muffins, as well as two bowls of Chinese crackers, though they were actually fireworks, so biting into one wouldn't have been a clever thing to do, no matter how hungry we were.

We set to eating, and for a moment I forgot about everything – even the Underworld – except how happy my belly was.

Stoop was in a cheerier mood when he'd eaten. He usually was.

Nancy and I took advantage by demanding that he tell us the truth. Stoop could see that **Resistance Was Useless**.

"If you must know," he said, taking a swig from a tankard of ale and stretching his feet to

* Or food, as it's better known.

the fire, "I grew up in Muckle."

"I didn't know you were from Scotland," I said. "You don't have a Scottish accent."*

"I haven't been back home in nearly two hundred years," said Stoop. "You can easily lose your accent in that time."

"Does your family still live here?" I said.

"Crabbit – that's my dad – does. He has a house on the harbour. It's called Dunmoanin. But don't get any funny ideas about meeting him. You don't pop in and say hello to someone after two hundred years."

"I'm sure I'd want to see Dad if I hadn't been home in centuries," I said.**

Stoop was adamant.

"Crabbit didn't want me to become a monster hunter," he went on sadly. "He said I wasn't big enough. In the end, I was left with no other choice. I ran away from home when I was seven to **Follow My Destiny**."

"So that's why you were so reluctant to

---

* Which was odd because Nancy did have a Scottish accent, and she'd never been here before.
** The longest we'd ever been apart was when he was kidnapped once by the aforementioned Aunt Prudence.

come here," said Nancy. "It wasn't because Lubbers aren't worth the effort."

"They're really not," said Stoop. "In fact, I'd bet my life that the Lubbers in Muckle Abbey are the exact same ones who used to live nearby when I was a nipper. But if you insist on wheedling out all of my secrets, then I admit it. The main reason is that I didn't want to come back to Muckle."

I decided to drop the subject. I didn't want to bring up any bad memories for Stoop.

Besides, my curiosity had been stirred by a newcomer who was standing in the doorway of the inn, pushing back the hood of his cloak and looking around as if in search of someone.

I'd never seen anyone like him before. He was all sharp angles, as if he'd been drawn by someone who'd never seen a curve. His elbows could have taken your eye out.

Stoop soon spotted the newcomer too.

"That's all we need," he sighed, taking another guzzle of ale and wiping the foam from his beard with the back of his sleeve.

"Do you know him?" I asked.

"I'll say I do," said Stoop. "That's Hatfield. A monster hunter by trade, though I don't recall him ever catching a real monster. I've not seen him for ages. What's he doing here?"

"Why don't you ask him?"

"Not a chance. Once he gets going, we'll be here all night. He loves the sound of his own voice. Let's beat it while we have the chance."

The chance never came. Hatfield's gaze fell on us, causing him to flash a smile so bright it was as if he had two rows of tiny lanterns in his mouth instead of teeth and had forgotten to turn them off to save electricity.

He swooped across the room to our table.

"My old friend, Poop!" he cried. "How delightful to see you again. What have you been up to since we last met? Do tell all."

# MMS

Stoop shoved back his chair, laid his hands flat on the table, and pushed himself up to his full height.*

"My name," he said fiercely, "is Stoop!"

"Is that not what I said?"

Stoop growled deep in his throat like a badger with a bad cough and no medicine.

"No. It. Isn't."

"You must accept my apologies," said Hatfield, taking a chair.* "I'm not good with names. When I received a distinguished service medal from the King of Lapland,

---

* Which, without wanting to be mean, wasn't very full.
** That means he sat on it, not that he literally took it, because that would be stealing.

in gratitude for my efforts in catching the Lesser Spotted Hoopdoodle, I couldn't for the life of me think what he was called. Then I remembered. It was 'the King of Lapland'."

He jiggled so hard with laughter as he took off his cloak that I had to duck my head to get out of the way of his pointy elbows.

"He was always boasting about that back in the day," Stoop whispered to me and Nancy as Hatfield helped himself to a Swiss roll. "Drove the rest of us mad. To be honest, I think he made up the Lesser Spotted Hoopdoodle. The rest of us have never seen one. It should be called the Never Spotted Hoopdoodle!"

He scowled across the table at Hatfield.

"What are you doing in Muckle?"

"I'm living here for the moment," Hatfield said. "I've been renting a room with an old chap called Crabbit down by the harbour."

Stoop spluttered so hard into his ale that the spray from his mouth nearly put out the fire.

"You'd better not be sleeping in my old bedroom," he declared.

"Now you mention it, I think I might be," Hatfield said casually. "The bed is VERY small and there are all these pictures on the wall of monsters scribbled badly in crayon, signed 'By Poop, Aged 6¾'."

"Stoop!" I corrected him in irritation.

I might as well not have bothered.

"Crabbit invited me to stay," Hatfield went on, ignoring me completely, "after I was called in to deal with a particularly troublesome Redcap in his basement."

"A Redcap?" said Stoop worriedly.

I didn't blame him for being alarmed.

Redcaps can be nasty, as *Monster Hunting for Beginners* makes clear.

# Redcaps

Redcaps are one of the most fearsome monsters in Scotland. They're so-called because they dye their hats in human blood. They have long teeth and sharp talons, both of which it's wise to keep away from, but they also wear iron boots, which are quite noisy on floorboards, so the good news is that you can generally hear them coming from a long way off and scarper. You can only defeat them by boiling them alive in hot oil. Not that you're allowed to do that, but it's worth bearing in mind if you're in a pickle. If you're in an ACTUAL pickle, then you have far bigger problems, because those things are impossible to escape.

hats covered in human blood

stained cape

long talons

steel boots

"If you did boil it in oil," said Stoop, "then I'm sorry, but I'll have to report you."*

"There was no need," Hatfield said. "I just used my natural cunning to scare it off. Crabbit was so glad of my help that, when he heard I was looking for a base for my new organisation, he begged me to move in."

"What organisation?"

Hatfield reached into his pocket and took out three small, neatly printed white cards, handing one each to Stoop, Nancy and me.

**MONSTER MANAGEMENT SOLUTIONS**
The fast, efficient answer to all your monster-related problems.
Call now for a free consultation.

* He didn't sound one bit sorry.

"I call it MMS for
short," he said.

"Monster Management
Solutions!" Stoop read out
disbelievingly. "I've
never heard anything more
ridiculous. You can't just set
up your own monster
hunting organisation."

"Yes, you can,"
retorted Hatfield.
"And I did, right after the
International League of Monster Hunters and
I, er, parted ways."

"But . . . but . . . it's against regulations."

"Rules are there to be broken, Droop."

"I won't tell you again! It's Stoop!"

"Is it? Then tell me, Gloop, who made
you the boss of monsters?"

"He has a point," said Nancy.

"He does NOT have a point," shouted Stoop. "He has the most point-free point in the history of points. I won't let him get away with this. I'll report him to Monster Hunting HQ in Llan . . . Llan . . . that town in Wales where Monster Hunting HQ is located."*

"That's another thing," said Hatfield, unconcerned. "Who wants an office in Wales, miles from anywhere? I'm in negotiations to set up branches in London, Paris, New York, possibly the South Pole too if I can find someone to put in some central heating."

"How on earth will you afford all that?" said Stoop in amazement, because property doesn't come cheap at the South Pole. Arthur was always moaning about the cost of holiday homes down there.

"That's easy," said Hatfield. "I've been charging a fee to get rid of monsters."

The whole inn fell silent as Stoop toppled backwards out of his chair in shock.**

---

* *Llanfairpwllgwyngyllgogerychwyrndrobwllllantysiliogogogoch. It used to belong to the Druids before they retired to take up ballrom dancing.*
** *I thought that only happened in stories.*

# Money Talks

It's not easy to shock someone who's been hunting monsters for two hundred years.

Stoop had been in the front line at the Battle of Nether Wallop when the last of the Fuddy-Duddies fired a fusillade of their own dung at the advancing army of monster hunters, creating a mound of droppings so high that the only mountaineer brave enough to try and climb it was still only halfway to the top.

"Not scared of a little competition, are you, Snoop?" said Hatfield, and Stoop was still so stunned that he didn't even correct him about his name. "If you want my opinion –"

"I don't!" said Stoop as he clambered back on

to his chair, rubbing the seat of his pants which had taken the impact when he fell.

"You're getting it anyway," said Hatfield, flashing another smile. "The International League of Monster Hunters has had things its own way far too long. I can offer a new approach. That's why I intend to ask this young lady to join me as I go forward."

"Jack's not a lady," said Stoop in confusion.

"I think he means me," said Nancy. "Though I'm not sure I like being called a young lady. It sounds a bit smarmy."

"My humblest apologies," said Hatfield . . . smarmily. "I happened to be down by the loch earlier and saw how well you dealt with those pesky Fog Goblins. It's clear to see that you are the brains of this outfit."

"I wouldn't say that," said Nancy modestly.

"Yes, you would," snarled Stoop. "You say it at least nine times on every adventure."

"You see? This is what I'm talking about,"

Hatfield said. "You're exactly the kind of young lady . . . I mean expert monster hunter . . . I've been looking for. You might even be the best new hunter of monsters since that girl in Tibet who made a household pet out of the Abominable Snowman. He's so tame now that he lets her tie ribbons in his hair and paint his toenails with glitter."

"You can't steal Nancy from us!" I cried, horrified at the thought of losing her.

"Goodness, you do strike a hard bargain," Hatfield continued. "Very well. I'll even double your wages, Nancy, if you agree to throw in your lot with me."

"I don't get any wages," said Nancy.

"No wages?" said Hatfield, pretending to be outraged. "In that case, I'll triple them!"

Nancy said she'd sleep on it and get back to him in the morning with her answer.

"You're not really thinking of joining Monster Management Solutions, are you?"

I whispered to her.

Nancy's secret smile gave nothing away.

Stoop looked uncomfortable – and not only because the leg of his chair had broken when he fell off so now it wobbled.

"Brains are all very well," he said defensively, "but they're not much use when an army of Fuddy-Duddies is firing fresh dung at you from their rear ends. What you need most in that situation is a large shovel – and absolutely no sense of smell."

Stoop flung out his hands to demonstrate the best method of defending yourself against a manure-launching monster, but he only succeeded in knocking the first bowl of uneaten Chinese crackers into the fire.

All at once, the fireworks exploded, shooting colourfully in every direction and filling the air with a stink of singed hair as Hatfield's eyebrows caught fire.*

"Save me, Stoop," begged Hatfield in a panic,

* In hindsight, putting fireworks so close to a fire hadn't been the Cleverest Idea Ever.

swatting his eyebrows as if they were angry wasps intent on stinging him to death.

"How many times do I have to tell you? My name is Poop!" exclaimed Stoop, picking up his tankard and throwing the last of the ale into Hatfield's face to extinguish the flames.

Stoop realised too late what he'd said.

The pleasure on his face at soaking Hatfield turned to embarrassment as the other guests in The Smuggler's Inn started chuckling.

"Did you hear what he called himself?" they sniggered.

Furiously, Stoop threw the second bowl of Chinese crackers into the fire as well, and laughed uproariously as everyone scattered to escape the fiery bombardment.

"Serves you right!" he bellowed at them, gesturing to us that it was time to go.

But he was still red with shame as the door closed behind us on our way out.

# Why Me?

Normally after a big meal, Stoop liked to have forty winks. A few more, if he could get them. Not tonight. He was eager to prove that he was still the best monster hunter in Muckle.

"What I don't understand," said Nancy as Muckle Abbey gradually came into sight again, outlined like a broken tooth against the stars, "is why the Sisters of Perpetual Misery asked for Jack by name. They must have a **Special Reason** for wanting YOU to deal with the Lubbers rather than some random monster hunter. What do you say, Stoop?"

"Your guess is as good as mine," the little man barked. "I don't know any more about those supper-hogging nuns than you do. The abbey wasn't even here when I was a boy."

"Not here? How could THAT great lump of stone not have been here?" exclaimed Nancy. "Look at it! You can tell it's really old. Some might say it's really, REALLY old. Maybe really, REALLY, REALLY old, and you can't get much older than that."*

"Not everything that looks old IS old," Stoop said carelessly, but I could tell that he was bothered by it too.

Was that why he'd looked so doubtful when he saw Muckle Abbey for the first time on the headland after the fog cleared?

Any chance to ask was cut off as the door of the abbey opened silently at our approach.

Stoop didn't even get a chance to add his own creak this time, and he made no bones of the fact that he was **Quite Cross** about it.

Nun The Wiser, who'd been awaiting our arrival, raised a finger to her lips and

* Unless it's really, REALLY, REALLY, REALLY old, but that's just being silly.

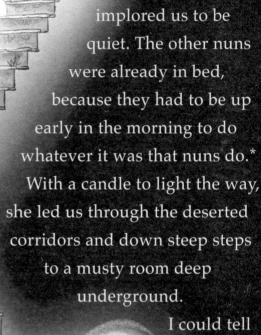

implored us to be quiet. The other nuns were already in bed, because they had to be up early in the morning to do whatever it was that nuns do.* With a candle to light the way, she led us through the deserted corridors and down steep steps to a musty room deep underground.

I could tell that it was a kitchen because there were brass pots and pans dangling from the ceiling, and a teetering pile of

* Nunning, I presumed.

dirty plates crusted with leftover steak and kidney pudding in the sink waiting to be washed up.

This, Nun The Wiser informed us in a low voice, was where the Lubbers always appeared on the stroke of midnight. No one knew where they came from because none of the nuns had dared spend the night in the kitchen to find out.

"Including me," she said with a shudder, "and I'm not about to start now."

Hurriedly, she bade us good luck, before retreating up the steps, taking the candle with her. The kitchen at once sank into gloom.

The three of us crouched under a table out of sight to wait for the Lubbers.

The only sound was the ticking of a clock as the minutes counted down to midnight.

Or was it?

"Listen," I said. "Something's coming."

# Lubber
# Party

From under our feet came the sound of scratching. It was getting louder all the while. Presently it was replaced by scraping.

Nancy nudged me and pointed to the middle of the floor where a flagstone was lifting up.

For a moment, I feared that the monstrous residents of the **Underworld** had grown tired

of waiting for the abbey to fall down and were coming to make an early start on **THE END OF THE WORLD AS WE KNOW IT.**

Then the clock chimed midnight, and out from the hole poured a legion of Lubbers. They looked exactly as they did in *Monster Hunting for Beginners*, but there were far more of them than could fit in a single picture.

In seconds, they were rampaging round the kitchen on their hooves, squealing with delight.

Some charged into the larder and came out carrying armfuls of bread rolls, and chicken legs, and slices of sponge cake, and jars of jam, and chocolate biscuits, and bottles of lemonade as big as themselves, and proceeded to sit down on

the floor for a midnight feast.

Others leaped in the sink to help themselves to the nuns' leftovers before throwing the dirty plates at each other like frisbees.

Lubbers, it quickly became clear, were not very skilled at throwing or catching, because they dropped most of them. The plates smashed to smithereens against the walls, with the Lubbers cheering at each new crash.

"Oh no you don't!" said Stoop, crawling out from under the table.

The Lubbers had been taken unawares, but they were more than a match for Stoop. They took one look at him and cried, "Look who's back in Muckle! It's **Grumpy Pants** himself."

Then they bolted.

Desperately, Stoop swung his arms round and round as if he was a windmill in a storm, but they were too fast to lay hands on.

They seemed to be enjoying the chase. Rather than escaping to safety, they kept darting forward until Stoop almost had them, then dodging nimbly out of his way.

"Almost got me that time, GP!"

"Try again!"

"He was a lot quicker as a kid, wasn't he?" they shouted in delight to one another.

Nancy and I tried to help, but they were such a blur that we could barely catch our breath, never mind a Lubber.

They were definitely trickier than Stoop had led us to believe.

Presently, the Lubbers got tired of the game, and made as one for the loose flagstone, slipping through the crack, taking as much food and drink with them as they could carry.

There was one left.

This was our last chance to nab him before he too vanished down the hole.

I waited for my moment . . . and leaped.

My hands closed round the Lubber.

"Got you!" I shouted.

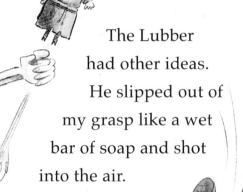

The Lubber
had other ideas.
He slipped out of
my grasp like a wet
bar of soap and shot
into the air.

Nancy dived to
the left and caught
him with one hand,
but the same thing
happened to her.

Up he rocketed again.
I dived to the right,
and grabbed hold of
him a third time.*

\* *Strictly speaking, it was only a second time for me, but a third if you include Nancy's catch.*

It wasn't until the fourth try that I was able to hold on to him for good.

"Put him in here," gasped Nancy, handing me an empty jam jar which the Lubbers had handily licked clean earlier.

I lowered the jar carefully over the Lubber's head, the way you might trap a spider to throw it outside.** It was a squeeze, but no matter how hard

** *Though actually you shouldn't throw them out at all, because every single spider eats at least forty bugs a day. That's more than 29,000 in the average spider's lifetime, and who wants that many creepy crawlies in their house?*

he pounded on the sides of his glass prison the Lubber couldn't get out.

Worse for him, the jar wasn't **COMPLETELY** clean, so he was getting blobs of jam over himself as he struggled and there's nothing ickier than sticky hands and hair.

"Let me out!" he pleaded.

"Not on your nelly," said Stoop, coming over to congratulate us on our joint efforts. "Not on anyone's nelly. Not even Nelly's, whoever she is." But we all knew the jar wouldn't hold the little creature forever.

Stoop instructed us to stay where we were to ensure the Lubber didn't make his getaway while he hurried to the larder to fetch a lid.

Nancy, the Lubber and I were left by ourselves in the now quiet kitchen.

That's when I noticed he'd stopped struggling and was crying instead.

# Lubber Talk

"I give up," he wailed, lifting up the corner of his habit and dabbing his eyes. "You win. You may as well kill me now and be done with it."

"What makes you think we're going to kill you?" I said, feeling bad that the Lubber thought I was the sort of boy who'd do something so awful in punishment for taking a few slices of sponge cake without permission.

"Why else would you capture me if not to kill me?" he said, lifting another corner of his habit and blowing his nose loudly into it.* "Make it quick, that's all I ask."

* *Urgh.*

He closed his eyes tight and dared us to **Do Our Worst.**

"We're really not going to kill you," I promised. "We just want you to stop being such a nuisance every night to the Sisters of Perpit . . . Pertip . . . Whatever-It-Is Misery.* They're miserable enough as it is without you stealing all their chocolate biscuits too."

"Stealing?" The Lubber was affronted, but at least it finally stopped him from crying. "We don't steal anything, Bill!"

"Actually, my name's Jack," I told him, "and this is Nancy."

The Lubber didn't care. Lubbers called everyone Bill, because it was easier to remember names when they were all the same.

That's why they were all called Bill too.

I made the Lubber slow down and begin again, determined to get to **The Bottom** of this riddle – or close enough to see **The Bottom** if we squinted hard, at any rate.

* When would I ever get their name right?

Piece by piece, the story came out.

It all started, Bill explained, when he and his fellow Lubbers were forced to leave the crumbling castle on a nearby hill where they'd lived for years, bothering no one.*

"There we were, Bill, sitting on the moor, getting cold and wet," the captured Lubber said, "when along came a **Mysterious Stranger** who offered to help us find a new home."

"Who is this **Mysterious Stranger**?" I said.

"Who's to say?" Bill replied. "That's what makes him both mysterious and a stranger. We called him Bill**, but we never actually saw his face because he always hid it under a hood. He's the one who showed us the tunnel into the abbey. He said we were welcome to live under the flagstones and gorge ourselves to our hearts' content on whatever we found in the pantry, and even smash all the plates if we felt like it."***

* Except for the neighbours disturbed by all the loud parties.
** That didn't surprise me.
*** Which they absolutely did.

"Why did this **Mysterious Stranger** want to make life so difficult for the Sisters of Perpetual Misery?" wondered Nancy.

"Beats me, Bill. It's not like we want to be here. We miss our castle terribly."

"Why not go back then?" I said.

"Weren't you listening?" said Bill. "We were **FORCED TO LEAVE.**"*

"By what?" asked Nancy.

Bill lowered his voice to a whisper. We pressed our ears to the side of the jar to hear.

"**Ghosts,**" he said.

* I can't have realised the importance of those three words first time round because they didn't have capital letters.

# You Know Whats

"**Ghosts**?" I exclaimed.

"Not so loud!" hissed Bill, as if the word had the power to make more ghosts appear.

"Sorry," I said. "I've never come across a gh– I mean, a You Know What before."

"You're lucky," he said. "They're not just scary. They're not just terrifying. They're SCERRIFYING."

He needed to say no more. I knew all about scerrifying ordeals.

"Naturally, we fled," he said. "We weren't staying to be haunted."

"So if someone can rid your castle of **You Know Whats**, you'll go home?" said Nancy.

"On the double," said Bill. "Why would

we want to stay here for the rest of our Lubbery lives? The food's a bit too rich for my tastes, Bill, and, between you and me, there's sometimes a **Terrible Stink** under the flagstones from somewhere down below."

I thought it best not to mention that the stench was probably coming from the monster-riddled **Underworld** on which Muckle Abbey was built. Bill seemed nervous enough.

Nancy and I looked at one another and nodded. We'd both had the same idea. If it worked, it would solve everyone's problems.

Well, not EVERYONE's, but everyone who lived in Muckle, which would be a start.

I asked Bill where this crumbling castle of his was to be found. Once satisfied that we had the right directions, I lifted the jar and let him go. He ran round happily in circles, thanking us repeatedly and promising that, if we were ever in a tight spot and needed help, the Lubbers would come to our aid.*

"I'm sure we won't need to do that before the

* Lubbers are loyal like that.

end of this adventure," I said optimistically as he skedaddled back down the hole, pulling the flagstone into place behind him, "but it's nice of you to offer all the same."

"Where's he gone?" said Stoop when he came back a moment later from the larder.

"He managed to knock over the glass and escape," I said. "We tried catching him again, didn't we, Nancy, but he was slippier than ever with all that sticky jam over him."

"He was our bargaining chip," grumbled Stoop. "I planned on holding him hostage until the other Lubbers agreed to our demands."

"You should have come back quicker then," Nancy said. "What took you so long?"

"I couldn't find the right sized lid," Stoop said shiftily, but the blob of whipped cream on the end of his red nose told its own story.

"You've been helping yourself to the sponge cake, haven't you?" I accused.

"Perhaps a slice or two," he admitted.

"A whole cake or two, more like," I muttered, knowing Stoop.

"I hope you're not suggesting this is my fault," Stoop retorted, eyes crossing as he stuck out his tongue in an effort to reach the last bit of cream.* "Let  me remind you, it was you two who lost our one and only Lubber."

"Surely trapping another one should be, er, a piece of cake to a mighty monster hunter like you," Nancy said with a grin. "You said it yourself. They're only Lubbers, after all."

A giggle from under the flagstones let us know that the Bills appreciated a joke almost as much as they liked lemonade.

*I don't know why he didn't use his finger. That's what I would have done.

# Don't Sleep On It

"Forget it. I'm not looking for ghosts tonight," said Stoop as we trudged back to Muckle and Nancy and I filled him in on the latest developments. "It'll be blacker than a raven's beak in that castle of theirs."*

"Not afraid of them, are you?" said Nancy.

"How dare you?" said Stoop. "My only fear is one day running out of cabbage. But it's late and I need my beauty sleep. I'm not even sure ghosts are real, but if they are then they'll still be there in the morning, won't they?"

By the time we reached The Smuggler's Inn, most of the lights in the village were out, apart

---

* Stoop could be very poetic when he put his mind to it.

from one or two in upper rooms. Our footsteps
sounded loud in the empty streets.

Nancy went to her room, and Stoop and I went
to ours. He instantly flopped down on his bed
and sank into sleep within moments.*

He snored so loudly that each fresh rumble
sent him a few inches down the bed.

I lay down on my own bed and tried to sleep.
It should have been easy. It was long after
midnight and I'd been awake for HOURS.

It was no good. I couldn't sleep without
reading a few pages of *Monster Hunting for
Beginners* first.

I didn't want to wake Stoop, because he'd be
even grumpier than usual if I did, and a more
grumpy version of an already permanently
grumpy Stoop would be too much grumpiness
to handle this late.

I skooshed down under the blankets, and
turned on the torch, but sometimes the book is
in a **More Than Usually Unhelpful Mood**,

* *He didn't even brush his teeth to get rid of the cake crumbs.*

and tonight was one of those nights.

*Have you ever seen a creature like a centipede, but ten feet long, with 1,000 legs instead of 100, bright blue needles for fangs, and a taste for children's innards? No? Well, you're about to, because one just crawled under the covers. Aaargh! Only kidding. It's actually twelve feet long. Aaaaaargh! Only kidding. Its fangs are actually bright orange. Aaaaaarrrrrgh! Only kidding. It has a taste for children's outtards too. Aaaaaaarrrrggggghhh! Only kidding. (I really am this time.) Sorry, I've never been able to resist a good practical joke.*

A cough outside in the street made me jump. I shut the book and switched off the torch.

Forcing myself to leave the safety of the blankets, I made my way gingerly to the window, stepping over Stoop who'd snored himself right off the bed and was now lying face down in a tangle of blankets with his bottom sticking in the air.

I peeked through a gap in the shutters.

Down below stood a figure, wearing a hood. I couldn't see its face, but it was definitely looking up at our window.

Could this be the **Mysterious Stranger** that Bill the Lubber had spoken about?

Curiosity won out over fright. I pulled on my boots and snuck out of the room, creeping downstairs to the front door of the inn and letting myself out, intending to catch the hooded watcher unawares.

There was nobody there.

# FSOS

"Psst!"

It sounded like a tyre had sprung a puncture, but I rarely brought my bike with me when monster hunting because it was too heavy to carry, so it couldn't be that.

The "psst" had been to get my attention.

"Nancy, is that you?" I asked the Nancy-shaped outline that suddenly appeared out of nowhere in the dark.

"You do ask some silly questions, Jack," came the answer as the glow from the street lamp fell on her face. "Who else do you know who looks exactly like me?"

"You might've been a Boneless," I said.

Nancy had never heard of that creature.

I took out *Monster Hunting for Beginners* and showed her the right page.*

# Boneless

*Sometimes the Boneless appears in the form of a fox. Sometimes it's a hippopotamus. Or a death watch beetle. Hummingbirds are a pretty common choice. As are the Billy Goats Gruff, saddleback pigs, ptarmigans, marmosets, newts, and Yorkshire terriers. It can even be a Tiddlefish when circumstances call for it. What I'm saying is that the Boneless can change shape at the drop of a hat, or the drop of an anything if you don't own a hat, so it can look like any creature at all. Nobody knows what its real shape is. Even the Boneless doesn't know who it really is deep down, which is*

---

* It would have been pointless to show her the wrong one.

quite sad when you think about it. But not as sad as you'll be if you meet one, since the only activity which helps the Boneless forget its inner sadness is killing everyone it meets. Here's a picture of a friendly little rabbit that might be a Boneless, but probably isn't.

long whiskers

long ears

small tail

"Let me get this straight," said Nancy after she'd read it. "A Boneless can be any shape?"

"That's right."

"Then how do you know I'm NOT a Boneless? I might be. I could've taken Nancy's shape to lull you into an FSOS."

"FSOS?"

"**False Sense Of Security**. That's what monsters often lull their victims into in order to make it easier to kill them."

"Are you a Boneless?" I said.

"That's for me to know and you to find out," she replied with a giggle.

It was good to hear her laugh.

A Boneless might be able to take on Nancy's appearance, but only Nancy could have made that Nancyish sound.

"What are you doing out here anyway?" I said now that I was sure she was harmless.

"I could ask you the same thing."

"There was someone out here, staring up at our window," I said. "I thought it might be the **Mysterious Stranger**."

"So that's why you were sneaking downstairs, is it? I knew you must be **Up To Something** when I heard you tiptoe past my door. I thought you were going to the castle to look for ghosts without me."

"I would never do that," I vowed.

"I should think not. But since we're both

here, why don't we go together?"

"Now?" I said nervously.

"No time like the present," said Nancy, who never took NO for an answer, unless NO was the answer that she was looking for, in which case she wouldn't take YES.

It started to rain lightly as we started out. I turned up my collar, wishing I'd put on my coat, but knowing that, if I went back to get one, I wouldn't have the courage to come out again.

We hadn't gone far when I realised it would be easier to find a castle in the dark and rain if we could see where we were going.

I switched on the torch.

Nancy grabbed my arm.

I grabbed hers.

Both of us gulped.

Up ahead stood a great beast, stamping its hooves, with flaming eyes and smoke billowing from its nostrils.

# Roll With It

What I'd normally do in such circumstances is check *Monster Hunting for Beginners* for advice on identifying and defeating our foe, but this was definitely not the time for reading.

The good news was that the great hoof-stamping, flame-eyed, smoke-billowing monster hadn't charged yet.

That gave us a moment after grabbing and gulping to study it more closely.

"Those aren't flames," said Nancy in due course. "It's the torch flashing in its eyes."

The nostrils weren't billowing smoke either. That was its breath in the cold air.

As for the stamping hooves, there was a far less chilling explanation.

"It's not a monster," I said, laughing with relief. "It's a horse."

The horse came trotting towards us through the rain, until it was close enough for us to reach out and stroke its wet mane.

Each time we stopped stroking it, the horse bumped us gently with its snout for attention.

I wasn't afraid.

I knew this creature couldn't be wild, because it was wearing a bridle round its neck. It was the nastiest looking bridle I'd ever seen, fastened together with metal studs like the ones Aunt Prudence used to have in her hobnailed boots, and with jangling chains for reins. But horses only wear bridles if they belong to someone.

"We have to go now, Horsey," I said after a while, wishing I could think of a better name, but eager to reach the Lubbers' ghost-infested castle before I lost my nerve completely.

Nancy and I tried walking round the horse.

It moved to block the path.

We went the other way.

It obstructed our way again.

"You want us to ride you, is that it?" said Nancy. "Not tonight. We have work to do."

The horse was insistent.

Maybe it was hungry?

I dug into my pockets looking for something a horse might like to eat.

In the left pocket was a lollipop that had been there so long it had melted and stuck to the lining. I'd need a chisel to get it off!

In the right pocket I found a sausage roll.

I always kept one with me in case I got peckish while out monster hunting.

I had no idea if horses liked the taste of sausage rolls, but who doesn't?

I held it out for this horse to nibble. It gobbled up the snack in two mouthfuls, then belched deeply with satisfaction.

I tried to think of it not so much as losing a sausage roll as gaining a friend.

"Can we go now?"

The horse stepped aside and let us pass, neighing softly as if in thanks. When I looked back again, it was nowhere to be seen.

It wasn't far to the castle from here. Out of the dark came a dismal moaning.

It might have been the wind, if there had been any wind, but there wasn't.

No prizes for guessing what it was.

OOOOOOHHHH!

Many monsters make unearthly wailing noises.
It's one of the commonest sounds monsters make.
   Take Howlers.

## Howlers

*Howlers are responsible for most strange noises heard
by travellers late at night on lonely roads, and even
on roads that have lots of friends. They also cry before
storms. Their ability at predicting the weather makes
them ideal for rehabilitation after being captured.
Many have gone on to become famous TV weather
forecasters, though why anyone should be famous for
announcing that there's a 36 per cent chance of rain
tomorrow is one of life's great mysteries.*

This wailing didn't come from
a Howler.

It drifted from the Lubbers' castle. Neat as
a pepperpot, it stood all by itself, as most
castles do, on a hill at the end of the road.
Nancy and I stepped through the entrance
and climbed the steps to an upper room with
nothing in it but a table and two chairs.

There wasn't even a ceiling, because it
had fallen down, letting the rain in.
The two chairs were occupied.

In stories, ghosts are often portrayed as
billowing white sheets with holes cut at eye
level so that they can see out. In real life, that's
not what ghosts are like at all. They're just
people who got stuck on earth after they died,
and they look like the ordinary people they once
were, except for being a bit more see-through,
as if made of smoke.

The two ghosts who were sitting
on matching chairs in the Lubbers'
castle, glimmering faintly from

122

within, weren't like that. They looked EXACTLY like they'd dressed up as ghosts for Halloween by wearing sheets with the eyes cut out.

You could have used them as tablecloths.

They were each taking it in turns to say, "Oooooooh!"

That was the wailing we'd heard.

"Oooooooooh!" said the first ghost.*

"Oooooooooh!" said the second.**

Then it was the second ghost's turn to start a new round of Ooooooooohs.

"Oooooooooh!" he moaned.

"Oooooooooh back at you!" responded the first one, with an extra "Oooooooooh!" for luck.

They really did enjoy Ooooooooohing.

"Oooooooooh!" they shrieked again when they saw us. "Don't sneak up. You scared us."

"We scared YOU?" I said. "We're the ones who should be afraid!"

*I called him that because he was closest to us.
**You can probably work out why I referred to him that way.

The ghosts looked at each other with as much puzzlement as a pair of sheets could manage.*

"Why would anyone be afraid of us?"

"Because you're . . . you know . . . ghosts," I said gently, in case they were still sensitive about . . . you know, again . . . being dead.

"We DO know, as it happens," said the second ghost. "Who'd know better than us? But we're not doing any harm. We just sit here, out of everyone's way, saying **Ooooooooooh.**"

Another round of **Ooooooooohs** ensued.

"I'm Mop, by the way," said the first ghost when they stopped **Oooooooohing** for a bit.*

"Thrilled to meet you, Mop By The Way," said Nancy respectfully.

"It's not Mop By The Way, it's just Mop. And I don't mean Just Mop. I mean Mop. And this is my good friend Mow."

"The pleasure is all ours," said Mow. "We don't get as many callers as we used to when we were alive. We'd offer you tea, but we don't have a fire to heat the kettle on."

* Which wasn't much, in all honesty.
** Constant Ooooooohing must be very tiring.

They both looked mournfully at the hearth, which was empty save for a heap of twigs topped with a bird's nest that had fallen down the chimney, with the bird still sitting in it.*

"It wouldn't matter if there WAS a fire to heat a kettle on," admitted Mop, "because we don't have a kettle either."

"Or any cups," said Mow.

"Plus, we can't drink," said Mow. "We tried it once, but the tea trickled down all the way inside us and made a puddle on the ground."

The rain coming in the roof was falling through them as they spoke.

Nancy and I sympathised, saying it must be very inconvenient** if that happened every time they wanted to quench their thirst.

We were having such a pleasant time it seemed a shame to reveal why we were there, but we owed it to the Lubbers.

"Go on," said Nancy. "Tell them."

* The bird was currently fast asleep, oblivious to the Ooooooooohs.
**And ticklish too.

# Scarier Than

# OOOOOOOHHHH

"What are Lubbers?" said the ghosts after I'd explained whose castle they were in.

I reached for *Monster Hunting for Beginners* to show them a picture, because it's so much easier to imagine what things look when there's a picture to go alongside the words.*

"Why, those are the little fellows who were here when we moved in," said Mop.

"So they are. It was most peculiar," Mow recalled. "We'd barely poked our heads through the door – literally through the door – when they all screamed and ran away."

"Things that AREN'T ghosts do tend to be afraid of things that ARE," Nancy said.

"But we're not even scary,"

*As anyone reading this book already knows.

*OooOooOOAH*

said Mop. "Do you think we're scary?"

Nancy had to admit that she didn't.

Even the **Ooooooooooohs** didn't
sound so dreadful now that we had heard
them up close.

I could probably have managed
a more hair-raising one myself.

I gave it a go.

"**Oooooooooooh!**"

*OOOOHHH*

Mop and Mow declared it a very good
effort for someone who wasn't dead, but I
suspect they were only being polite.

"**Ooooooooooooooooooooooooooh!**" added
Nancy, producing the most impressive one yet.

I was slightly scared myself, despite
knowing she wasn't a ghost. Mop and Mow
congratulated her warmly and said she
was welcome to come and join them in the
**Ooooooooohs** any time she wanted.

"The thing is," I said, "this is the Lubbers'
castle. Their dearest wish is to come back and
live here again, but they can't because you're

here, and they're afraid of you. It's not their fault. They haven't had the chance to get to know you as well as we have. I hate to ask, but isn't there somewhere else you could go?"

"**Oooooooooh**, but there was," said Mow. "We had a lovely home, didn't we, Mop? Had it furnished nicely, exactly the way we like it."

"You should've seen our curtains. We often wish we were as colourful." Mop looked wistful. "It can get boring being a plain ghost. Patterned spooks have much more fun."

"There you are then," said Nancy. "If you go back to your house, the Lubbers can return here, and everything will be as it was."

"But that's what we're trying to tell you," Mop and Mow said together. "We can't."

They promptly informed us how their peaceful existence in the house with nice curtains had been shattered by an **Unearthly Wailing** outside their bedroom window.

"More unearthly than Nancy's **Oooooooooooh?**" I asked.

"Far more unearthly."

"That IS unearthly," I said

"Night after night it went on," said Mop. "We couldn't sleep a wink."

"And if we don't get a minimum of ten hours," said Mow, "we wake up all wrinkled. You should have seen the state of us. We didn't even have an iron to smooth us out."

"What was making the moaning?" I said.

"We can't say for certain, but we think it was the **Loch Less Monster**."

I frowned. Something about the ghosts' story was **Not Adding Up**. Stoop said Lessie had been living in Loch Less for hundreds of years. Why would she suddenly start wailing so loudly that it stopped ghosts sleeping?

Unless something had disturbed HER too . . .

"Who told you it was Lessie making the noise?" Nancy enquired.

We should have known what was coming next. It was the same **Mysterious Stranger** who'd tricked the Lubbers into thinking they were welcome at Muckle Abbey.

"He assured us that this castle was empty, so we moved in at once," said Mop, "only to discover it was swarming with Luggers, or whatever you call them. We were quite ready to share – we're not proud, are we, Mow? – but they fled before we could say hello."

For the second time that night, Nancy and I exchanged glances as we thought of a plan.

Strictly speaking, it was Part B of the same plan, but all that mattered was whether it worked, not what it was called.

"Are you saying, if we can get Lessie to stop wailing outside your window each night, you'll return to your house, and the Lubbers can move back in to the castle?" I said.

"We guarantee it," said Mop. "We can't possibly stay here now we know it belongs to someone else. We thought those little fellows had just popped in on a sightseeing tour."

That was all we needed to know.

# Three's a Crowd

I woke the next day to find Stoop standing next to my bed, shaking his head disapprovingly.

"You missed breakfast," he said. "What kind of self-respecting monster hunter misses breakfast? I'll tell you what kind. The kind who misses lunch and dinner, that's what kind. Then where are they? Missing supper too, I shouldn't wonder. It's a slippery slope, Jack."

"I had a sleepless night," I yawned, but Stoop wouldn't let me finish.

"You had a sleepless night?" he cried. "I woke up face down on the floor with my backside sticking in the air. That is not a good position in which to sleep, let me tell you."

Once Stoop got going, he could grumble for hours. I waited until he paused for breath before springing out of bed and informing him about our much more exciting evening.

"So you see," I finished, "all we have to do is find the Loch Less Monster and ask her to stop wailing, then Mop and Mow can go back to their house, and the Lubbers can return to their castle, and the Sisters of Potpip . . . Prepop . . . Peepot – oh, you know who I mean! – won't have to leave Muckle Abbey, and everything will be the way it was before."

"You went to the castle without me?" Stoop demanded when I was done. "You're an apprentice, Jack. You're not supposed to go off on **Dangerous Missions** without an experienced monster hunter at your side."

"Mop and Mow aren't dangerous."

"You didn't know that at the time, did you?" he reminded me. "It clearly states in the *International League of Monster Hunting* regulations that *Beginners* and *Not Quite Beginners* must be accompanied by a fully qualified instructor at all times. And that's me. I have badges to prove it and everything."

"I'm sorry," I said, not wanting to fight. "Nancy and I were only trying to help."

"Nancy, Nancy, Nancy!" huffed Stoop. "That's all I ever hear these days. If you ask me, that girl is a **Bad Influence**."

"What did you call me?"

We turned to see Nancy standing in the doorway, with her arms folded, listening.

If anything, that just made Stoop stubborner.*

"I said you're a **Bad Influence**, and I meant it," he said. "In fact, I hereby forbid you from taking part in all our future adventures, Nancy. I don't have a contract with you. My agreement's with Jack. You're only . . ." – he fumbled for the right word – "the sidekick."

"Nancy isn't a sidekick," I exclaimed.

*I've no idea if that's a real word, but it should be.

"You bet I'm not," said Nancy. "You're just jealous because I beat you at arm wrestling last week. Seven times in a row."

"I went easy on you."

"She also saved you when that **Giant Crab** picked you up by the beard and tried to drop you in a bottomless well," I reminded him. "You'd have been **Done For** if not for Nancy."

"**Giant Crabs** or not, my mind's made up," said Stoop. "I agreed to take you on. **Not** her. It wasn't a **Buy One Get One Free** offer."

"You didn't AGREE to take me on at all. You tricked me, in case you've forgotten?"*

"That's neither **Here nor There**," insisted Stoop. "Well, maybe it's a bit more **There** than **Here**, but either way I'm not budging."

"It's not fair to make people pick between their friends," I said sadly. "It's like asking you to choose between lunch and dinner."

"Talk to the beard, because the ears ain't listening. But don't take too long deciding,"

*That's all explained in my first adventure too.

Stoop added. "If you want to find Lessie and ask her to stop wailing, so that the ghosts can go back to their cottage and the Lubbers to their castle, then you'll need a boat – and I happen to know the very boat for the job."

I looked from Stoop to Nancy . . . and from Nancy to Stoop . . . but all that toing and froing didn't make my decision one bit easier.

It only made my neck sore.

"It's OK, Jack," said Nancy eventually. "You can go without me."

"Really?" I said, because, if there was one thing that Nancy loved, it was being in the thick of the action.

"Really," she said. "It's your duty as a monster hunter to find Lessie and

make everything right again. I'll wait here till you get back. You can tell me all about it then."

I felt dreadful about leaving her behind, but what else could I do? Saving the day had to be my **Top Priority**. Glumly, I put on my boots and followed Stoop down to the harbour.

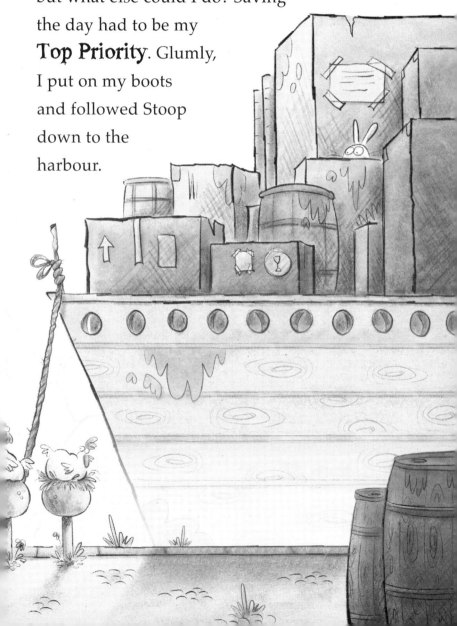

# Sick as a Budgie

As it turned out, there was only one boat anchored in Muckle harbour anyway.

It was called the *Great Haul,* and it was piled high with barrels and padlocked trunks with **HANDS OFF** written on the side.

Standing on deck was a young woman in a tricorn hat. She had on a long coat with shiny buttons that hung open to reveal the baggiest trousers I'd ever seen. Six people could have fitted in each leg and still left enough room for a friend.

"Meet Rochester," said Stoop. "She's the smuggler whose inn we're staying at. I met her this morning at breakfast when I was tucking into my fourth bowl of sausages. Or it may have been the fifth. I lost count."

"My brother tells me it was the sixth," said Rochester, sweeping off her hat in greeting so that her long hair tumbled out. "He's had to order an extra delivery for tomorrow."

"I expected you to have an eyepatch, a wooden leg and a parrot," I admitted.

"You're thinking of pirates," she said. "People often make that mistake."

"Is there a difference?" I asked.

"I'll say. Pirates are cruel and bloodthirsty. Do I look cruel and bloodthirsty?"

I assured her that she didn't.

"A parrot would be

good company on long smuggling trips," she conceded. "I did once own a budgerigar, but he suffered from motion sickness whenever the boat left harbour, so I have to leave him behind now with Crabbit."

"Never mind that," snapped Stoop impatiently, changing the subject as he always seemed to do when his dad was mentioned. "Rochester, we need your boat for an hour or two on monster hunting business."

"What's in it for me?" said Rochester.

Once again, Stoop flashed his gold card from the *International League of Monster Hunters*, and offered to let the smuggler borrow it for two afternoons in the next month* in return for use of the *Great Haul*.

"As much free cabbage as I can eat?" said Rochester. "How can I say no? Hop aboard."

Who'd have imagined there was someone in the world as keen on cabbage as Stoop?

*Three if she really insisted.

# All Hands on Deck

Half an hour later I was standing on deck in the middle of Loch Less being squeezed into a diving suit, ready for my encounter with Lessie.

"There was none of this mollycoddling when I started out," Stoop said, tightening the fastenings to make sure the suit wouldn't let in water once I was submerged. "I was thrown in the deep end. Literally. A merman had taken up residence in the local pool and was putting all the customers off by making **Sarcastic Remarks** about their swimming abilities when they dived in. I was handed a trident, pushed in the water and told to chase him out."

"Why a trident?" I said.

"Because that way I looked like Neptune, God of the Sea," Stoop replied as if the answer was obvious. "He's the only thing mermen are afraid of. Apart from mermaids, but that goes without saying. Even Neptune's scared of them. It's all in the book."

## Mermaids

*Mermaids can often be seen sitting on rocks, combing their hair and singing songs to tempt lovesick sailors into flinging themselves into the water to be with them. This makes mermaids laugh themselves silly for hours, especially if the sailors drown, which they generally do, not being able to breathe underwater. The only activity mermaids like better is roasting freshly caught mermen over an open fire, though they do tend to squabble over who gets to eat the tastiest bits. If they're lucky, the roasting mermen can take the opportunity to* untie themselves and swim to safety, though that does risk making the mermaids cross. If they catch the fleeing mermen, they don't even bother roasting them, but eat them raw.

You might wonder how they're able to keep a fire burning at the bottom of the sea. I can't answer that. I'm here to tell you about monsters, not underwater impossibilities.

long hair

eyes on stalks

gills

no legs

webbed fingers

"You don't think there are mermaids down there, do you?" I said, staring into the murky water for a glimpse of a fishy tail.*

"You'll have bigger problems than mermaids to worry about if Lessie catches you," said Rochester.

"You can keep that nonsense for the tourists," said Stoop. "I've already told Jack that Lessie's not dangerous. I don't even believe she's the one behind the **Unearthly Wailing**. She never used to do it. True, she topples the odd fisherman into the water for fun, but who doesn't like swimming?"

"You," I said. "That's why it's me inside this diving suit."

Stoop insisted that I had nothing to worry about. Most people who went diving underwater did come back up again.

Eventually.

They weren't always alive when they did, he added grudgingly, but it was their own fault for not following instructions.

*Though if I had seen a fishy tail, it may only have been a fish.

"We'd better run over them one more time then," I said as he lifted the diving helmet on to my head and screwed it into place.

"It's simple," he said. "This tube here, attached to the helmet, provides you with oxygen. But there isn't a limitless supply in the tank, and I don't want to have to pay for a refill, so don't stay down too long. When you want to come up, tug on the tube and we'll do the rest. Got it?"

"I think so," I said, but a lot of things happened between the "I" and "so".

I'd got to "I" when something bumped violently against the bottom of the boat. Instantly, I was pitched head first off the edge.

I was halfway between the deck and the water when I reached "think" – and it says a lot about what came next that this was still probably my favourite bit of the experience.

By the time I made it to "so", I was already underwater and sinking fast.

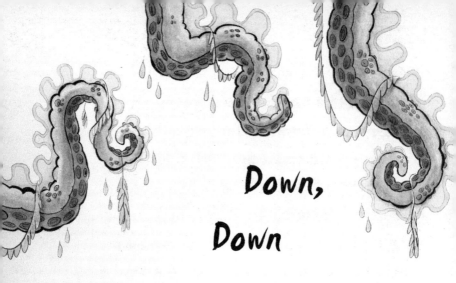

# Down, Down

I'd thrown stones into water many times.

It's always fun to see how far you can fling them, or how big a splash* they make when they hit the surface. But I'd never considered what happens to the stone AFTER you lose sight of it. At that moment, I was finding out. The stone was me, sinking down.

And

    down.

        Then

           down

                some

                    more.

*Or even a sploosh if you're very lucky.

At first, I had no control over where I was going. I spun round and round like a starfish as I fell, limbs sticking out in different directions.

Slowly, I slowed.

I began to get used to the sensation of being surrounded by water.

Soon I could hold myself upright, though I still wasn't sure that I WAS the right way up.

It was too dark to see anything save for an occasional fish who peered in the window of my helmet as if I was a goldfish in a bowl.

Presently, I became aware of a light glimmering somewhere beneath me.

It was coming from a city.

I'd have pinched myself if I wasn't trapped inside a diving suit. Instead I blinked hard to make sure I wasn't seeing things.

If I was, the blinking made no difference, because the city was still there when I stopped.

It had been built on a lump of rock, with grand buildings at the top, and squares and houses laid out below, lights shining in every window, and winding streets filled with strange creatures going about their daily business.

At least they looked strange to me, though to them it must have been me who looked peculiar, floating down from a liquidy sky. I wished Nancy was there to see them.

Strangely, the inhabitants of the city didn't seem to be scared of me. Their shrimp-like eyes, which were attached to the end of stalks, were wide with excitement not terror.

As I came to rest on the bottom of the loch, they came streaming out of the city's main gate onto the sand in a long procession, headed by their leader who was dressed in a shimmering gown made from silver fishscales with a crown of fishbones on her head.

Rather than hands, she had pincers like a crab, and she held them up in greeting as she opened her mouth to speak, bubbles streaming from her like a string of soap suds.

"Hail, Great One!" she declared.

# Bad Air Day

"I think you must be mistaking me for someone else," I said as the inhabitants of the city bowed down low before me. "I'm not a **Great One**. I'm a **Quite Good One** some days when it comes to monster hunting, but I still have lots to learn. Call me Jack."

"Don't be so modest," the one who'd first hailed me said, a further jet of bubbles rippling from the back of her gown, like when your bottom decides it wants to join in as you're singing in the bath. "I am Borborygmus, Most Gaseous Ruler of the Loch Creatures, and we have awaited this glorious day for centuries, ever since it was foretold that a hero would

come to save us in our hour of peril."

"If you have any perils to deal with, I'd be more than happy to help," I said. "But I really think you're wrong about the **Great One** thing. What makes you so sure it's me?"

"Our ancestors drew a picture of the **Great One** so we'd know we had the right one when the hour arrived," said Borborygmus. "We'd never live it down if we hailed the wrong one. Bring forth the portrait!"

The crowd of **Loch Creatures** parted, and out from the gate came one of their number, wearing a '**Great One Fan Club**' T-shirt and carrying a large portrait between his pincers.

He held it up in triumph.

As one, the inhabitants of the city bowed down low before me, flurries of bubbles escaping from their nether regions too.

"That's not me!" I said.

"**The Great One** jests," said Borborygmus. "It's exactly like you. Look, the face on the portrait has a nose. You have a nose. It has a chin. You have a chin. It's right there below your mouth. What more proof do you need?"

"It has three eyes!" I said.

The **Loch Creatures' Most Gaseous Ruler** gazed from me to the picture, and back again, a trace of doubt showing on her face.

"He only has one more eye than you," she said at last. "That's not many more."

"But it IS more," I said. "Plus, the face in the picture isn't wearing glasses like I do. And he's bald. I have hair. You can't see it at the moment because of the diving helmet, but you'll have to take my word for it. It's very messy. **The Great One** also has floppy ears like a basset hound. They're really nice ears, but not like mine. Come to think of it, I'm fairly sure that's a picture of a monster."

"The artist who drew this likeness may have used **Artistic Licence**," Borborygmus said, "but it's close enough for us. Tell us what to do, **Great One**. What is your command?"

I wasn't the LEAST BIT comfortable pretending to be a mighty hero whose coming was foretold centuries ago, but perhaps I could make these peculiar creatures' faith in me work to everyone's advantage.

"Please don't think of it as a command," I said. "It's more of a request. You see, I'm looking for the Loch Less Monster, and I'd be grateful for any clues you could give me about her **Present Whereabouts**."

The Loch Creatures suddenly seemed VERY interested in a passing shoal of fish.

"The Loch Less Monster, you say?" said Borborygmus. "I'm afraid we have no information on her current schedule."

"Have none of you seen her?"

The Loch Creatures shook their heads, and the bubbles from the back of their clothes went into overdrive with nervousness.

Then one of them gave a panicky cry, and all their eyes twitched on stalks as they swivelled in the same direction. I turned my head to see what they were looking at.

There, fast approaching the city through the murky water, was Lessie.

# GIVING CHASE

Lessie must have seen me. I was hard to miss in my diving suit. She made a sharp U-turn and fled back the way she'd come.

Surely the Loch Less Monster wasn't afraid of ME? Whatever had made her run, this was my one chance to catch her.

It wasn't easy to move fast in the diving suit. It wasn't easy to move ANYWHERE underwater. I probably wouldn't have kept up with her at all if it hadn't been for the tube leading from my helmet back to the boat.

As I spun round to see where Lessie had gone, it flicked sharply like a whip, propelling me through the water faster than a harpoon.

Luckily, it sent me whizzing in the same direction as the monster.

"Come back!" yelled Borborygmus.

Not a chance.

I managed to grab on to Lessie's tail and was dragged along behind her through the gloom. Frightened fish scattered in every direction if they saw us coming, or were sent flying like brightly-coloured skittles smashed into by a bowling ball if they didn't.

"Watch where you're going, road hogs!" they gurgled after us disgruntledly.*

Lessie tried jerking one way, then the other, to shake me loose, but I held on fast. Once I let go, that would be the end of the pursuit.

I only hoped the line connecting me to the boat didn't snap or run out before Lessie reached her destination. (Wherever that was.)

Several bubbles of worriment escaped from the back of my diving suit.

At last, Lessie seemed to be reducing speed.

*I don't think that's a real word either, but it's too good not to use.

She wasn't gyrating as madly as before, and her flippers weren't flipping so flipping fast.*

Looking ahead, I saw we were heading towards another huge rock like the one on which the Loch Creatures' city sat, only this one had an opening at the base.

In a final effort to dislodge me, Lessie swooped steeply and dived through the opening, dragging me inside after her, before coming to a rest on the sandy floor of a grotto whose walls sparkled with minerals.

Why had the Loch Less Monster brought me here? I gulped in anticipation, and the back of my trousers produced more bubbles.**

What she did was nothing at all.

Lessie didn't even move.

That, I discovered as I put my hand to her side to make sure that she was still alive, was because Lessie wasn't a monster.

* I presumed that's what flippers did. If they flapped, they'd be called flappers.
** Strictly speaking, the bubbles came from me, not the trousers.

# Lessie's More

Lessie's skin didn't feel like skin.

It was cold and hard to the touch.

When I rapped my diving gloves on her side, she gave off a hollow sound like a biscuit tin with no biscuits inside.*

In short, Lessie was a submarine.

To be strictly accurate, she was a submarine which had been wrapped up to look like a water monster, with flippers sticking out, and humps running down her long back, and a tapering tail at the rear, and large circular eyes at the front which were actually lamps to light the way ahead in the murky water.

The submarine had an engine to make it go,

*The very worst kind of biscuit tin.

and a window at the front so the Loch Creature operating Lessie could see out when driving.

The tiny pilot was sitting in the cockpit, grinning at me anxiously through the glass, as if wondering how hot under the collar I was about being hauled through Loch Less like a blobfish on the end of a fishing line.

I was more baffled than bad-tempered.

"Who are you?" I cried in wonder.

"I'm Flatulous," the pilot said, opening the window and climbing out so we could stand as face to face as you can stand with someone who's a hundred times bigger than you are. "Captain of the Good Ship *Fake Lessie*."

"Submarines are actually called boats, not ships," I felt compelled to point out, having once read that particular fact in a book.

"I didn't know that," said Flatulous, with a rush of bubbles from both ends to show that she too was well named. "We'll rename her the Good Boat *Fake Lessie* at once."

"I don't understand," I said. "Why are you

pretending to be the Loch Less Monster?"

"You have discovered our greatest secret," said the voice of Borborygmus, as the body of Borborygmus from which it issued swam through the entrance into the grotto.

The Loch Creatures had followed us from the underwater city, though, having no engines of their own save for bubble power, it had taken them a little longer to make the journey.

"The truth is," the **Most Gaseous Ruler** confessed, "there is no Lessie."

"No Loch Less Monster?" I said. "That can't be true. Stoop told me she was real."

"Lessie did live here once," said Borborygmus. "She was our absolute favourite monster. She protected our city from harm. But she always complained that the water was too cold for her Delicate Constitution. One day she packed her bags and swam off in search of tropical climes. We were sorry to see her go. But not as sorry as we were terrified."

"Scerrified!" burbled the Loch Creatures.

"What did Lessie protect you from that was so scerrifying?" I asked.

"The Muckles," they all said at once.

"They're so big and loud," said Borborygmus. "We had to think of something to keep them away once Lessie was gone. Flatulous suggested building a submarine and pretending to be a monster so the Muckles would be too scared to come out on the loch."

"So it was you who bumped into the boat earlier, making me fall in?" I said.

"Sorry. We didn't know you were the **Great One** back then."

"Don't start that again," I said.

"You do see, though, don't you?" said Flatulous. "Once the Muckles knew that Lessie was no more, they'd have been out on the loch all hours of the day and night, disturbing us with their outboard motors, tossing rubbish over the side. We couldn't allow it. We had to do Something Drastic while we awaited a new hero to protect us."

"Now we don't need to," said Borborygmus. "You're here to save us, even if it's true that you don't really look like the ancient picture."

"The resemblance isn't even close," the others muttered under their bubbly breath.

"Stop it!" I said. "I can't be your Great One. I only came down here to beg Lessie or you or whoever's doing it to stop making the Unearthly Wailing outside Mop and Mow's house so that the ghosts can go home."

Flatulous insisted she'd never done any wailing with the Good Boat – formerly known as the Good Ship – *Fake Lessie*.

"The submarine is designed for **Stealth and Speed**, not **Unearthly Wailing**," she said. "There's not even a setting for **Earthly Wailing**. What makes you think it was us?"

I couldn't answer Flatulous's question. But if it wasn't Lessie who'd driven the ghosts from their house, then who was it?

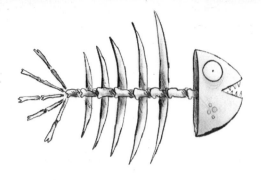

# No Blabbermouth

One tug on the line later and Stoop and Rochester were hauling me on to the deck of the boat as if I was a weird fish they'd landed.*

Hastily, I removed the diving helmet, and helped myself to an enormous gulp of air, as Stoop demanded to know why the boat had suddenly shot off across the water a while ago like it was attached to a torpedo.

"I'll tell you later," I whispered as I climbed out of the rest of the diving suit.

"Put your mind at ease, Jack," said Rochester, overhearing. "I can guess what you're going to say. Lessie's not real, is she?"

*Mainly Rochester, because Stoop was quite small.

164

Stoop guffawed.

"That's a good one," he said. "You'll be saying your baggy trousers aren't real next."

He stopped guffawing when he realised that we weren't guffawing along.

"I've suspected it for years," Rochester confessed. "That's the reason I tried to put you off from jumping in the water, Jack, by telling you Lessie was dangerous. If I was right and there WAS no monster, I didn't want everyone else finding out. It would be bad for trade. Why else do you think I put up those warning signs along the shore? As long as people in Muckle are afraid to leave the harbour, I have the loch to myself. It's ideal for smuggling."

"Why didn't you just say no when we asked to borrow your boat?" I said.

"And miss out on free cabbage?" she said.

Stoop regarded Rochester with new found respect. Here was someone with a love of leafy, green vegetables to match his own.

His mood soon changed when I begged him not to add the **Loch Creatures** to *Monster Hunting for Beginners,* or every monster hunter in the world would instantly learn of their existence and Borborygmus and her bubbly-bottomed people would never get any peace.

"What do you take me for?" huffed Stoop. "I'm not a tattletale. I'm not a snitch. I'm certainly not a **Blabbermouth**, because they're a rare species of **Tree Spirits** found only in the tropical forests of central Tonga. This does throw a spanner in the works all the same. We can't complete our mission if we still don't know what's making the **Unearthly Wailing**."

"You mean an **Unearthly Wailing** like THAT?" I said with a shiver as a **Horrifying Howl**\* began drifting across the water.

*\*That's another way of saying Unearthly Wailing.*

# Having a Wail of a Time

The noise was like a thousand cats yowling and scraping a violin at the same time, while ten thousand owls shrieked at them to shut up.

I wanted to stuff wax inside my ears to stop it sending me **Stark Raving Mad**, and MY ears are earwaxy enough as it is.

"What is that racket?" moaned Stoop.

"I've heard it a few times when out on Loch Less lately," said Rochester. "I just thought the wind wasn't feeling well."

Whatever it was, the wailing was getting louder and more unearthly the closer that we drifted to shore, until it filled the air the way the smell of someone breaking wind fills a lift.

Through trees, I glimpsed a small cottage

with brightly patterned curtains at the window.

"That must be Mop and Mow's house,"
I yelled at Stoop over the noise, but he
couldn't hear. **The Eerie Bawling**\* was
too loud now.

Rochester pointed out a dark figure standing
on the shore below the house.

At first I thought it must be the **Mysterious
Stranger**, but this one didn't have a hood.
Then I saw more figures all dressed in the same
hoodless way and arranged in a circle.

It was the Sisters of Perpetual Misery, and
they were . . .

"Singing!" I gasped.

Suddenly everything became clear.

So THIS was the **Unearthly Wailing** that
had driven the ghosts from their home.

No wonder Mop and Mow had fled! The nuns
were even worse at singing than Dad was at
cooking.\*\* Listening to them trying to carry
a tune was more painful than being rolled on by

* That's yet another name for Unearthly Wailing.
** I wouldn't have believed that was possible until now.

a whole family of **Kerfuffles**.

"Make it stop!" was all Stoop could say.

As if in answer, the song abruptly ended, and my ears were filled with relief like your nostrils are with fresh air when the door of the stinky lift finally opens and you can escape.

We watched in silence as the nuns all closed their hymn books and walked in single file back to Muckle Abbey.

I could have jumped up and down for joy, if it wasn't for the risk of leaping right back into the water, this time without a diving suit.

"The mystery is solved," I said to Stoop as we watched them depart. "True, we still don't know who the **Mysterious Stranger** is, or why he encouraged Bill and his friends to make Muckle Abbey their home, but that can wait. Our job was to get rid of the Lubbers under the flagstones, and now we know how to do it. All the Sisters of Whatchamacallit Misery have to do is stop holding choir practice next to Mop and Mow's house, and the ghosts will be able to go home, and the Lubbers can return to their castle, and the nuns won't have to leave Muckle Abbey, thereby avoiding THE END OF THE WORLD AS WE KNOW IT."

What could be easier?

You can probably tell by the number of pages to go that it wasn't quite so simple.

# Friends Disunited

There was a crowd waiting on the harbour when we got back to Muckle. Stoop thought it was a welcoming committee, and began preparing a speech on **The Life And Times Of A Great Monster Hunter**, before noticing that nobody was paying him one bit of attention.

Instead they were gathered round an angular and all-too-tall man with shining teeth.

"I should've guessed," said Stoop.

"How long will you be gracing our humble village with your amazingness?" the adoring locals were shouting at Hatfield.

"Do you have a message for your fans?"

"What, in no particular order, are your three favourite igneous rocks?"

"What's going on?" said Stoop, pushing his way through the crowd to reach Hatfield.

"Soup, my dear friend," exclaimed Hatfield, drawing back his hood as he turned to face him.* "You'll never guess what I've had to deal with while you were out playing on the loch. Behold . . . the Boneless!"

The crowd held its breath to see what fearsome creature Hatfield had trapped.

He held up a small cage in which sat a creature that looked remarkably like . . . a rabbit?

It sat there quietly munching on a carrot.

"That's a rabbit," said Stoop.

* Soup was a Big Improvement on Poop, so Stoop didn't bother correcting him.

"It looks like a rabbit, I do admit," said Hatfield. "But I'm assured that this is in fact a Boneless. As you know, they can take any shape whatsoever, including that of a rabbit. This one might have turned vicious at any moment if I hadn't enticed it into the cage with the very carrot you see before you."

The crowd murmured its approval of Hatfield's brilliance, before screeching in terror as the rabbit stopped chewing briefly to lift a back foot and scratch lazily at its ear.

"Who told you that scrawny critter was a Boneless?" said Stoop contemptuously.

The rabbit didn't care for the old monster hunter's tone and instantly threw the rest of his carrot through the bars at him.

Stoop caught it in midair and popped it in his mouth with a crunch.

"If you must know," said Hatfield, "it was Monster Management Solutions' newest – and indeed only – recruit. Here she comes now."

"You!" I exclaimed, as Nancy strode up casually to take her place at Hatfield's side.

"Hello, Jack! Hi, Croop!" she said cheerily.

"Don't you start," Stoop growled.

"You really did join MMS then?" I said.

"Why not?" said Nancy. "Sloop made it perfectly plain this morning that there's no place for me in your gang, so I decided to take Hatfield up on his offer of a job."

"And what a splendid addition to the organisation Nancy's already turned out to be. She's going to make me – or should I say, us – a small fortune. Or better still, a big one!"

Hatfield beamed at her proudly.

The crowd gave a round of applause in appreciation of his gleaming teeth. They'd never seen anything so bright in Muckle before. Up here, sunlight was just a rumour they'd heard about but never quite believed.*

"What say you and I head off to find more rabbits that we can pass off as Bonelesses . . .

* No wonder Lessie had left!

I mean, round up another batch of these ferocious beasts?" Hatfield said to Nancy, and she readily agreed.

"I'm sure I spied lots of them earlier at the other end of the beach," she said. "They were right next to that big rabbit warren."

"That's because they're rabbits!" snarled Stoop. "I used to play with them as a kid."

Nancy giggled.

"Don't be silly, Gloop. Why would anyone pay us so much money to catch some rabbits?"

I waved unhappily as Nancy and Hatfield hurried off to drum up more business for Monster Management Solutions.

I couldn't help feeling hurt that she'd chosen such an idiotic person over me.

But then hadn't I picked Stoop over her?

If only I'd stuck up for her back at the inn, Nancy would never have joined forces with Hatfield. This WHOLE mess was my fault,

"Don't blame yourself," said Stoop as the

crowd on the harbour began to break up. "I wouldn't be where I am today if I took responsibility for things that were my fault."

I thought about where he was today, which was grumpy and living in a shed. But I didn't say anything. Stoop always seemed content enough in his own strange fashion. I just didn't want to be like him in two hundred years' time.

I resolved there and then that, as soon as this mission was over, I'd find Nancy and beg her to come monster hunting with us again.

I didn't care what Stoop said.

He had a **Trick One, Get One Free** deal whether he liked it or not!

# Woe is Them

The Sisters of Perpetual Misery didn't take the news as well as I'd hoped. Some of them even began **Wailing Unearthily** again as Stoop and I stood in the candlelit hall trying to explain.

"Don't you see?" I said. "Once you stop singing outside Mop and Mow's house, everything will go back to the way it was before and you won't have to leave Muckle Abbey."

Hearing it again only made them cry more.

I wondered if the Sisters of Perpetual Misery were living up to their name, or whether it was knowing that they themselves had brought about the entire situation with the

Lubbers which was upsetting them.*

"We're sorry it's time for you to depart, that's all," explained Nun The Wiser. "We never dreamed you'd complete your mission so fast. We thought it would take longer. At least until half past eight tomorrow morning, or better still nine o'clock on the dot."

"What's happening at nine o'clock tomorrow morning on the dot?" I said, my suspicions roused.

"Nothing at all," she replied innocently.

"Indeed not," the other nuns joined in. "Nine o'clock has not the slightest significance to our plans. Whatever made you think it did? Forget we mentioned it."

"I already have," said Stoop, who couldn't wait to get away. "Let's get out of here, Jack."

That set the nuns off wailing again. They surrounded me and Stoop, begging us to stay.

"The thing is, Jack," said Nun The Wiser, taking hold of my elbow and pulling me aside where she could talk privately, "we haven't

* That's what's known in stories as Irony.

been entirely honest with you. Please don't think we're ungrateful after all your splendid monster hunting efforts, but the truth is that the Lubbers are not the only monstrous foe we face here at Muckle Abbey. That's why the Sisters are in such a skittish mood. An excess of fear has turned their minds to mushy peas."

"Fear of what?" I said.

"I hardly dare say its name," said Nun The Wiser. "But if you absolutely insist, I will. I'm talking about . . . er . . . the **Considerably-Sized Beast of Muckle Moor**."

The nuns let out a collective shriek.

Nun Of The Above
covered her
ears.

Nun Whatsoever fainted clean away.

"I've never come across such a creature in all my days," said Stoop, stepping aside so he didn't get flattened by another swooning nun. "And there are more than seventy-three thousand days in two hundred years so I'm sure I would have done."

"I give you my word that the **Considerably-Sized Beast of Muckle Moor** is very real, and absolutely not something I made up in an effort to stop you leaving," said Nun The Wiser. "Sisters, tell them about the Beast."

# Beastly Tales

The nuns all started talking at once.

**The Beast**, they declared, had a head like a scorpion . . . or it might have been a toad.

It had feet like a bobcat . . . or possibly a Russian wolfhound crossed with a baboon.

It had teeth of iron . . . or teeth of stone . . . or no teeth at all because it preferred to suck its victims to death like a leech.

It had feathers.

It had scales.

It slithered like a snake.

It scurried like a spider.

They said so many things that didn't make sense it's almost impossible to draw a picture of it. You'll have to imagine what it looked like, if you can. The one thing they agreed on was that it was **Considerably-Sized**.

Stoop suggested we look in *Monster Hunting for Beginners* for further details.

A quick glance under B for **Beast** and C for **Considerably-Sized** failed to find it.

I even looked under 'Muckle', 'Moor', 'The' and 'Of' to be extra sure.

"Take my word for it," said Nun The Wiser, ignoring the fact that we clearly didn't intend to take her word for anything or we wouldn't have double checked. "Each time it comes down from Muckle Moor, that **Considerably-Sized Beast** brings terror, the like of which has never been seen before. Everyone, please tell them more stories about the Beast that are definitely true and not huge whoppers."

Once more, the Sisters of Perpetual Misery described the ordeals they swore they'd suffered at the hands . . . or paws . . . or claws

. . . or hooks . . . or mandibles . . . of the **Considerably-Sized Beast** of Muckle Moor.

"It ate my big toe!" said Nun Too Soon.

"That's nothing," Nun Too Pleased butted in. "It ate both of my little toes, and together that adds up to more toes in total."

"It tried to drag me down the plughole one night in the bath," said Nun Of This.*

"It DID drag me down the plughole," said Nun Of That.** "And there wasn't even any water in the bath at the time."

"What did she do to you?" I asked Nun Of Your Business.

"None of your business," she said.

I should have guessed.

"She bit off my head!" yelled Nun Other.

Nun The Wiser scowled at her in disappointment, as if to say, 'You've gone too far, Nun Other. They'll never believe that.'

We didn't.

* Or it may have been Nun Of That.
** Or it may have been Nun Of This.

"I don't know what your game is," said Stoop, "but Jack and I are leaving this instant and none of your **NUNSENSE** can stop us."

"Wait!" said Nun The Wiser. "I admit it. The other nuns and I did exaggerate a teensy bit, but that's only because we've been so terribly afraid on account of the prophecy."

"Not another one," groaned Stoop.

"Yes, another one," said Nun The Wiser. "In my experience, ancient prophecies are like bookmarks. You can never have too many of them. And this is one of my favourites. For it is written that if the **Considerably-Sized Beast** of Muckle Moor is not defeated by tomorrow, it will mean . . . **THE END OF THE WORLD AS WE KNOW IT!**"

# Temptation Strikes

"This is getting silly," I said. "You can't keep saying everything will lead to **THE END OF THE WORLD AS WE KNOW IT** and expect people to believe you."

"It WAS a bit of a long shot," admitted Nun The Wiser, "but we had to try. You're absolutely sure you don't want to go up to Muckle Moor and fight the Beast?"

"Absolutely, definitely, categorically not."

"Fair enough," said Nun The Wiser after a brief hesitation in which she seemed to be considering her **Next Move**. "But please let us give you something as a token of thanks for solving the mystery of the **Lubber Invasion**."

"I don't want it, whatever it is," said Stoop.

"Not even lunch?" said Nun The Wiser.

"Did you say . . . lunch?"

"It's the least we can do to show our gratitude for all your help."

"I thought you were forbidden from eating with people who aren't members of your order?" I butted in. "You told us it was the first of the **Three Golden Rules**."*

"We're allowed to make an exception on Wednesdays," said Nun The Wiser.

"But it isn't Wednesday."

"Saturdays are acceptable too as long as they're one of those Saturdays that fall between Friday and Sunday. Look, do you want something to eat or not, Stoop?"

"I do!" said Stoop.

For someone who said his mind couldn't be changed, it had been changed as easily as if it was a light bulb that Nun The Wiser had unscrewed and replaced with a new one.

There was no use resisting.

* *She did say it too. It's on page 64.*

I consoled myself with the thought that lunch wouldn't take long.

Stoop was a fast* eater.

We were led into the refectory, which is what dining rooms are called in old abbeys, and the nuns proceeded to bring in dishes and platters and bowls and crocks and flagons and basins and thimbles and wheelbarrows and old sinks and paddling pools and any other receptacles they could lay their hands on, all filled to the brim with boiled cabbage, as if they'd been preparing for this moment.

I didn't like boiled cabbage**, but I had no idea where my next meal was coming from, so I reached for a bowl anyway.

Nun The Wiser rapped me on the back of the knuckles with a spoon.

"Nun for you!" she said. "In order to sit down and eat with the Sisters of Perpetual Misery, the Sixth Rule states that you must be at least . . ." She stopped. "How old are you?"

"Ten."

---

* Not to mention messy.
** I don't know anyone else who does apart from Rochester and Stoop.

"What a shame," she said. "You have to be at least eleven."

I was made to sit and watch as Stoop munched greedily on cabbage until his teeth were greener than stink bugs.

The nuns were watching him too. All their eyes were fixed on him as if waiting for something to happen.

Stoop paused mid-chomp when he realised that he was the centre of attention.

"What are you staring at?" he said. "Have you never seen someone eat cabbage before?"*

"Stoop," I said as the reason the nuns were eyeballing him started to become clear. "Are you sure you're feeling well?"

"Never felt better," he said. "I'm fit as a fiddle, and fitter than a flea. In fact, I'd gladly challenge any flea to a fitness contest. Go find me a flea and I'll prove it. Why do you ask?"

"Because you're going green," I said.

---

* To be fair, they'd probably never seen anyone eat it so eagerly.

# Unreasonable Demands

Stoop's whole face had changed colour. He looked like a sprig of broccoli. Even his nose, which had always been bright red, was green.

"Spoke – too – soon," he groaned. "Something – not – right. Cabbage – off."

He slumped face down into the bowl.

Panic-stricken, I shook Stoop desperately by the shoulder, shouting his name, but he didn't stir.

"You killed him!" I said in horror.

"He's not dead," said Nun The Wiser. "It would take more than a dodgy bowl of cabbage to finish off Stoop. He's merely sleeping, thanks to a few sprinkles of Nun Whatsoever's special dozing draught."

"That's why you didn't let me eat it," I realised. "It wasn't because I'm ten."

"Certainly not. That rule only applies to nine and unders. But we couldn't let you fall asleep too, Jack," Nun The Wiser said, eyes glinting slyly. "We have a special task set aside for you. We just needed Stoop out of the way first. We couldn't risk him doing something tiresome like trying to save you."

So that was it.

I'd be given some impossible challenge, like going to the **World's End** to steal the tail feather of a golden vulture. Or finding the one lamp with a genie in a cave piled high with thousands of identical lamps before the sand ran out in a hour glass.

If I failed, we'd both be for the chop.

How had I not seen the badness in Nun The Wiser until now?

Very well. Whatever task Nun The Wiser set . . . no matter how deadly or dangerous . . .

I was ready to undertake it to save Stoop.

Unless it was killing the **Considerably-Sizeᴅ Beast of Muckle Moor**, naturally.

The ban on slaughtering monsters applied to the ones who'd been made up as well.*

"Out with it!" I said. "What is the task?"

Nun The Wiser leaned in closely.

"The task we have set you . . ." – she paused dramatically while Second To Nun performed a drum roll on an upturned colander to build the tension – "is to spend the night here in Muckle Abbey as our special guest."

"Is that it?" I said, because it didn't sound like a difficult task compared to stealing golden tail feathers or finding magic lamps.

"That's it," she said.

"What if I refuse?"

"Be warned, Jack," said Nun The Wiser. "If you don't agree to our demands . . ."

She trailed off menacingly.

"Let me guess," I said. "It'll be **THE END**

---

* *Why should they be the only ones denied protection?*

**OF THE WORLD AS WE KNOW IT.**"

"What a peculiar thing to say," said Nun The Wiser. "Why would the world come to an end because you didn't agree to spend the night in Muckle Abbey?"

"Because that's what you always . . . oh, never mind. Go on then. What will happen if I don't agree to your **Unreasonable Demands?**"

"Your grumpy friend with the shaggy beard and green-but-formerly-red nose will remain face down in cabbage **For All Eternity**."

It didn't sound so terrible when she put it like that. Sleeping and cabbage were his two favourite things. Knowing Stoop, he might be more displeased if I DID wake him up.

Of course, I knew that I had to save him all the same, even if it did mean preventing him from living his best life. But how could I?

I was their prisoner.

"Don't think of it as being a prisoner," said Nun the Wiser. "Think of it as being locked up and unable to leave until we say so."

"Isn't that the same thing?" I said as I was carried away.

Clang

I was frogmarched* to the highest tower in
Muckle Abbey to pass the hours until nine
o'clock tomorrow morning on the dot.

"Make yourself at home," said Nun
The Wiser.

"How can I make myself at home in this
nasty, filthy, horrible pigsty?" I demanded as I
was led through the door, shutting my eyes to
the repulsiveness that awaited me inside.

"How dare you call my room a pigsty!" cried
Nun Of The Above.

I opened my eyes.

The room was **Quite Nice**. There was even
a bed with freshly laundered sheets and a new

* Not by actual frogs, I should say to avoid confusion.

195

quilt, topped with three fluffy pillows, some scatter cushions, and a teddy bear.

"Sorry," I said to Nun Of The Above. "I should've looked before insulting your room."

"Humph!" she said, which is a noise people make when they're not happy with you but don't want to get into a **Big Fight** about it.

Nun The Wiser took the opportunity to usher out the rest of the nuns and shut me inside, promising again that she had **Nothing Sinister** planned for the morning, so there was no point doing anything foolish like trying to escape.

"I'll be as foolish as I like," I insisted defiantly. "You try stopping me!"

I rushed at the door to attempt a **Daring Getaway**, only to hear the key turn in the lock.

Undeterred, I rattled the handle anyway.

Stoop had made the noise of a creaking door when we first arrived at Muckle Abbey. Maybe one of the Sisters of Perpetual Misery liked to imitate the sound of a key turning?

No such luck.

The door really was locked.

Heavy footsteps echoed as the nuns trooped down the stairs.

I was alone.*

The only other way out was through the window, but it was too narrow, as I found out when I got my head stuck in the gap and had to spend the next ten minutes pulling it free.

Even if I had squeezed through, I'd immediately have fallen a hundred feet to the ground, and that would not have been an **Obvious Improvement** on my situation.

There had to be SOME way of getting out of here which didn't involve being splatted stickily on the rocks below.

All I knew is that I had to try, because when someone says they have **Nothing Sinister** planned for you in the morning, that generally means they have **SOMETHING VERY**

* Apart from the teddy.

**SINISTER INDEED** planned, and it's best not hanging around to find out what it is.

I sat on the edge of the bed, swinging my legs to help me concentrate as I tried desperately to think of a way to save Stoop from his **Cabbagey Fate** and myself from whatever Nun The Wiser had in store for me.

# CLANG!

Was that what I thought it was? A hasty glance under the bed confirmed the worst.

The nuns had left me a chamberpot in case I needed the loo. I was determined not to use it, no matter how **Desperate For Relief**.

It would have been too **Embarrassing** if the Sisters of Perpetual Misery had burst in unexpectedly when I was sitting on it.

I'd just started wondering if I could use the chamberpot as a weapon instead when the keyhole in the door started whispering.

# Too Wicked for Words

"Magic keyhole, do you have a message for me?" I said with excitement, crouching down by the door and putting my ear to the hole.

"I beg your pardon?" came the reply.

"That's strange," I said. "You sound exactly like Nun The Less."

"I am Nun The Less," said the voice. "I'm here on the other side of the door."

"That does make more sense than a magic keyhole," I admitted. "What are you doing here? Won't the others be angry if they catch you talking to me without their knowledge?"

"Not half. I don't dare think what they'd do to me, but I had to risk it," Nun The Less said. "I only joined the Sisters of Perpetual Misery because I like the outfits. They're so stylish but practical. I had no notion in those days how bad Nun The Wiser was. What she has planned for tomorrow morning is so thoroughly wicked that it must be stopped."

"What IS she planning?" I said.

"I can't say," said Nun The Less. "It's too wicked for words. It's too wicked even for the words that were invented to describe the most wicked things. Don't make me say them."

I agreed that I wouldn't.

She HAD to help me all the same.

"Can't you fetch the key and let me out?" I asked.

"It's impossible," she said, shaking all over.* "Nun The Wiser keeps it on a chain round her neck, and she never sleeps these days. She just lies awake all night, sighing, 'What have I

---

* I couldn't see her shudder, because she was on the other side of the door. I just knew she did.

200

done? What have I done?' Is there no one else who can help you?"

I tried to think.

Stoop was drugged. Nancy was working for Hatfield. Dad was too far away.

"I've got it!" I said, snapping my fingers because that was what people always do in stories when they've **Got It** too. "Get word to Rochester. You can't miss her. She has a three-cornered hat and the baggiest trousers you've ever seen.* Apparently it's the fashion among smugglers. She's bound to come when she hears I need help. Please, will you go to Muckle at once and find her for me?"

"I'll try."

Dad always says the most important thing in life is to **Try Your Best**. Stoop says that's stupid, and what counts is not trying but succeeding. I didn't want to be disloyal, but I crossed my fingers that Nun The Less took after Stoop's philosophy rather than Dad's.

---

* Not that I knew how many types of trousers Nun The Less had ever seen.

# Fluff is Enuff

One hour later, I was starting to lose hope.

Two hours later, I'd lost it as surely as a ballpoint pen and some shiny coins down the back of the sofa. Had the visit from Nun The Less been an elaborate prank to make me believe I might be rescued, only to make it more upsetting for me when I wasn't?

Worst of all, I had to use the chamberpot. Twice.

I couldn't hold on any longer.*

I was hungry too, and began to regret giving my last sausage roll to the friendly horse last night. There was nothing to eat except for the

---

* I was pleased to say the nuns didn't burst in.

lollipop in my left pocket.

I used the chisel which I helpfully found under Nun Of The Above's pillow to chip the lollipop free of the lining in my pocket, together with a thick layer of fluff, and lay on the bed sucking it slowly to make it last.

The fluff gave it extra flavour.*

All the time I knew that I was **Delaying The Inevitable**.

I could put it off no longer. I had to read the section at the back of *Monster Hunting for Beginners* about the **Fiery Pits of Doom**. Biting my lip nervously, I opened the book at the warning I remembered so well.

*Read On At Your Own Peril!*

I turned the scorched page.

* *Now I think of it, I should probably have used the chisel to try and escape.*

> *You did see the bit about reading on at your own peril, yeah? Just want to check, because there's no going back if you continue now.*

I flipped another page.

> *Seriously, this is your last chance to think again.*

This was getting annoying.

> *Don't say you weren't warned.*

I skipped the next few pages in case there were more warnings, and immediately wished that I hadn't. The pages started glowing as if with fire, and my eye fell on some of the most scerrifying monsters imaginable.

There were Puckles and Haggles and Skullduggers, each more hideous than the last.

Some had no skin, so you could see their insides oozing out. Others had teeth so sharp that the very pictures had torn the page.

Each one of them looked as if they wanted to climb out of the book and devour me.

I tried to close it, but the pages themselves had grown hot. They burned my fingers, and I had no choice but to keep looking.*

Here are some more of the monsters from the **Underworld** that the book contained.

## Collywobbles

*When someone says they're suffering from an 'attack of the collywobbles', what they usually mean is that they're feeling scared or queasy for some reason. The real reason is that they've been attacked by actual Collywobbles.*

---

* I could have shut my eyes but I didn't think of that at the time.

big nostrils

little wings

big mouth

sharp spikes

This is what Collywobbles look like.

Yes, I'm afraid they are that ugly. Not everything in the world can be in with a chance of winning a beauty contest. You should see what you look like first thing in the morning before judging anyone else.

# Malarkey

You'll know when a Malarkey is nearby because they smell like a bin filled with dog food that's been covered with sour milk and then left outside in the sun for too long. Nobody knows why they smell that *way. It is known that they love rolling around at least once a day in a big bathtub filled with dog food, before washing their hair with sour milk and sitting out in the sun for long periods, but that's probably just a coincidence.*

There was a final message too.

*I bet you wish you'd listened to those earlier warnings now.*

The book wasn't wrong!

To think that these grotesque creatures were dwelling not far beneath my feet in the **Fiery Pits of Doom**, and if I didn't get out of here and stop the nuns' **Evil Plan** then Muckle Abbey might fall and set them all free.

What I couldn't have guessed is that the book had another **Unpleasant Surprise** in store.

On the very next page, I saw a familiar pair of flaming red eyes staring out.

# Flicker
# and Out

The horse that Nancy and I met last night HAD
been a monster. Its name was the Noggle.

## Noggles

*Unlike most horses, Noggles live mainly in water.
Never, ever take a ride from a Noggle, even if your
feet are very sore from walking and the idea of a
ride back into town seems appealing. Once you
climb on to its back, you'll be stuck like glue and at
the Noggle's mercy. And Noggles have no mercy.
Their chief delight is in dragging victims* down
*to their underwater lair and feasting on them. The
most effective method of overcoming a Noggle is by
combing its mane. This sends them to sleep, at which*

*point you should chop*
*off their head. It's*
*against the rules*
*but you can't*
*take chances*
*with Noggles.*
*Another way is to*
*remove the Noggle's bridle,*
*thus putting it under your*
*control. It will do anything you*
*demand to get the bridle back.*

So much for me thinking the bridle meant it
was tame! I couldn't believe I'd given my last
sausage roll to such a fearsome creature.

Or . . . was it the sausage roll that had saved
Nancy and me?

I wanted to find out more about the Noggle,
but the book sprang shut like a snapping
jaw, plunging the room into darkness as the
glowing pages were snuffed out.

I fumbled for my torch and switched it on.

The light flickered once.

Twice.

Went out.

More unnerved than ever, I curled up on the bed and pulled the new quilt over me, wondering how much of the night I had left to face.

I shouldn't have been able to nod off with so much to fret about, but I'd only had a few hours' sleep last night, and Nun Of The Above's pillows were **Extremely Comfy**.

My eyelids shut as tightly as a shop entrance at closing time.

Seconds or minutes or hours later – I've never been good at counting when I'm asleep* – I jerked upright at the sound of a voice on the other side of the door.

"Stand back and take shelter!" it bellowed.

"Take shelter from what?" I said groggily.

The answer came immediately.

* Or awake in school.

# Not Banana or Marzipan

The blast hurled me through the air as if the Fog Goblins were playing Hoo-Shank again.

I was in luck. I landed on the mattress. I checked to make sure I was in one piece, which is generally accepted by most doctors as the best number of pieces for a body to be in.

The count didn't reach two, so that was a bonus. The teddy hadn't been so fortunate.

I covered him gently with what was left of the quilt, then ran to thank Rochester for answering the call for help, because who else could it be who'd rushed to my rescue?

It wasn't the smuggler with the three-cornered hat and baggy trousers who climbed through the

**Gaping Hole** left by the bang.

"Nancy!" I cried. "What are you doing here?"

"What does it look like I'm doing?" she replied smartly. "I'm saving my best friend from a bunch of mad nuns."

"Who are you calling mad?" said Nun The Less, crawling into the room after her.

The blast had obviously knocked her off her feet too.

"I wasn't referring to you," said Nancy, helping Nun The Less to stand upright again. "Of them all, you're by far the unmaddest."*

"But Nancy, I thought you were on Hatfield's

* *That wouldn't be hard!*

212

side now," I said, unsure if the explosion had damaged my memory.

"You have a lot to learn, Jack," Nancy said. "I only pretended to join Monster Management Solutions to get my own back on you for letting Stoop make you choose between us. **Friends** should never do that."

"I understand that now," I said. "I really am sorry."

"Then let's say no more about it. Thankfully, everything turned out for the best," Nancy said. "Not only did I gather enough evidence to expose Hatfield as a **Big Phony** with that ludicrous scheme to catch fake Bonelesses, I'd also never have discovered his **Hidden Stash** of dynamite if I hadn't gone to work for him. What a monster hunter could possibly want with so many explosives is **Another Matter All Together**, but I'm sure we'll find out before the end."

"We usually do," I agreed.

"I'm glad he had some, all the same," she continued. "When you didn't turn up for dinner at The Smuggler's Inn last night, I knew something bad must have happened. Stoop would never willingly miss a meal! Then I heard Nun The Less telling Rochester you'd been taken prisoner. I immediately took charge of **Operation Free Jack**. I stole a few sticks of the dynamite and a box of matches and came here to put them to **Good Use**."

She gazed round proudly at the destruction, before pulling a face.*

"What's that smell?" she said.

I saw through the settling dust that the contents of the chamberpot had exploded all over the walls when the dynamite went off.

The freshly laundered sheets had sheltered me from the worst of the splatter, but fresh wasn't the word to describe them now.

Stained? Yes.

* It was her own face in case you're wondering.

Stomach-churning? Absolutely.

Yuck? Without question.

"It must be the dynamite," I said, hurriedly trying to change the subject.

"Nope," said Nancy. "Dynamite smells like banana or marzipan. I'm picking up an aroma of both. The other pong is more like –"

"Never mind what it's more like," I said, interrupting before her nose recognised it. "Shouldn't we be getting a move on, getting Stoop, and getting out of here?"

Grudgingly, Nancy agreed to put off a discussion of the **Awful Stink** until we'd also rescued the sleeping monster hunter.

I picked up *Monster Hunting for Beginners*, pleased to see that it hadn't been blown to pieces.* Then I tucked it in my belt for safekeeping and we made a break for it.

Halfway down the stairs, we met Nun The Wiser dashing up them the other way.

* Or stained by the insides of the chamberpot.

# The Chase Is On

Nun The Wiser held out her arms to prevent us passing down the narrow stairwell.

"Did you really think you'd steal Jack from us so easily?" she said to Nancy.

"It wasn't THAT easy," said Nancy. "I still have splinters of door in my hair."

"As for you, Nun The Less" – Nun The Wiser shook her head – "I'm disappointed in you. You know how important today is to us."

"Because of the anniversary, you mean?" said Nancy triumphantly.

"How do you know about that?" demanded Nun The Wiser. "Did you tell her our secret,

Nun The Less?"

"No," the timid Sister shrieked.

"Actually, I read about it in a leaflet I picked up at the tourist office in the village yesterday," Nancy said. "Muckle Abbey appeared one year ago this very morning."

"Nine o'clock on the dot, I bet," I said.

"You bet correctly," said Nun The Wiser. "And we intend to celebrate the anniversary in style. It's too late to stop us. Listen, the blast has brought the other nuns running. Hear their heavy footsteps! You're trapped."

"Not if I have anything to with it!" said Nun The Less, timid no more.

She launched herself at the head of the Sisters of Perpetual Misery like a half-eaten nut getting even with a greedy squirrel.

Both nuns went tumbling down the stairs, rolling over and over* until they reached the bottom in an untidy heap. Nancy and I shot after them to provide **First Aid** to Nun The

---

* *And over some more.*

Less if she needed it – and Nun The Wiser too, if we absolutely had to, though we'd rather not.

Both were already springing to their feet.

The three of us set off running again, this time with Nun The Wiser in pursuit.

Soon she was joined by Second To Nun . . . and Nun Too Soon . . . and None Other . . . and None Whatsoever. (I don't need to list them all again. You know who they were.)

Nun Of The Above was last. She'd gone up the stairs first to inspect her nice room and was furious at the state of it.

"What is that ghastly smell?" she said, as she joined in the chase.

"I don't know," shouted Nancy over her shoulder as she ran, "but it did smell awfully – and I do mean AWFULLY – familiar."

"Can we please talk about this later?" I cried, afraid that I'd never live it down.

In and out of doorways we sprinted, and round pillars, and under arches.

Sometimes we got separated from each other and found ourselves in the middle of the chasing pack, or following them instead of the other way round, and we all had to stop and swap places, apologising for the confusion.

"Coming through!"

"After you."

"No, after you. I insist."

"Don't you insist with me."

"I'll insist with whoever I like. What are you going to do to stop me?"

"Please, Sisters, no more fighting!"

"She started it."

"Did not!"

"Did so!"

"Can we please play hopscotch now?"*

In the end, there was only one door we hadn't tried. Growing tired, we burst through it to reveal a mighty chamber with something **ENORMOUS** rising up in the middle from floor to ceiling, as if it was holding up the roof.

* *It was hard to keep so many nuns focused on the Task In Hand.*

The mysterious **Enormous Something** was covered in a cloth, concealing its shape.

"Over there!" said Nancy, pointing to an exit at the far side of the chamber.

"Where?"

"There!"

"By the chair?"

"As far as I'm aware!"

Somehow in the confusion our feet got entangled and we tripped.

I flung out my hands to break the fall, and caught the edge of the cloth, pulling it loose.

It unfurled and fell like a great sail gliding to the deck of a ship when the ropes are cut, burying the three of us underneath.

Frantically disentangling ourselves, I looked up in horror at what it had been covering up.

It was a massive statue of Aunt Prudence.*

* Now you know why I kept mentioning her earlier.

# Things Get Worse

Aunt Prudence was the **Chief Villain** in my first adventure. She'd attempted to take over the world, as **Chief Villains** have a habit of doing, which is why she was now in prison.

I thought I'd seen the last of her.

Yet here she was, large as life.

To be exact, she was **LARGER** than life, because the statue of her filled the hall from floor to ceiling. What was her gigantic likeness doing in Muckle Abbey?

The other nuns stumbled to a stop when they saw Aunt Prudence in all her grisly glory.

"Behold Nun The Worse!" they cried, throwing themselves to the ground at her stony feet.

"What did you call her?" I said.

"Nun The Worse," repeated Nun The Wiser. "She's the REAL head of our order. I'm only standing in for her while she's Otherwise Disposed. We wear THESE in her honour."

As one, the Sisters of Perpetual Misery got up off the ground, lifting the bottom of their black robes to reveal identical hobnail boots of the kind worn by Aunt Prudence.*

"Those boots were the one part of the outfit I always hated," said Nun The Less. "The hobnails gave me blisters. That's why I've secretly been

* That explained all the heavy footsteps.

wearing these instead."

She lifted up her own robe to reveal a pair of pink, fluffy slippers on her feet.

"These are what helped me sneak up to Jack last night without being heard," she revealed.

The other nuns inhaled in horror.

"Wearing slippers is bad enough, but what you did, Jack, is unforgivable," said Nun The Wiser, grabbing my shoulder. "Because of you, Nun The Worse is no longer with us here at Muckle Abbey where she belongs."

"That's her own silly fault," Nancy retorted.

"We'll have to agree to differ on whose silly fault it was," said Nun The Wiser. "It's too late for us to reconsider the whole back story now. Why else do you think we lured you up here to Scotland, Jack? From the moment we found out what had befallen our beloved Nun The Worse in King's Nooze, we vowed to have our revenge."

"What are you going to do to us?"

I demanded.

"You'll find out," said Nun The Wiser. "Nun Whatsoever, fetch the dozing draught!"

Struggle as we might – and we did – the others nuns easily held down Nancy, Nun The Less and me, covering our noses with cloths soaked in the same foul smelling concoction which had sent Stoop into an unnatural sleep.

I tried to resist, but the medicine was stronger. I gave a stupendous yawn, and the lights in my head went out.

# Things Get Worser

When I opened my eyes, I was stranded in shallow water, strapped to a pole.*

There were two more poles, one on either side. Nancy was fastened tightly to one of them, and Nun The Less to the other.

Nun The Wiser stood at the edge of the loch, impatiently looking at her watch.

"About time too," she said when she saw the three of us waking up. "I told Nun Whatsoever to go easy on the dose, but she gets carried away sometimes."

*By that, I mean a big stick, not a person from Poland.*

"What are you going to do to us?"
I demanded, as I'd already done in the
last chapter without getting an answer.

On this occasion I did get an answer,
though it didn't make me feel better.

"We're going to sacrifice you," Nun The
Wiser said. "You first, Jack. Then Nancy.
And Nun The Less last of all. We were going
to sacrifice you all at once, but decided it
would be more fun to do it one at a time."

I gulped. Of all the things Nun The Wiser
could've said she was going to do, being
sacrificed was among my least favourite
options.

"You don't have to do this,"
I pleaded.

"We know," said Nun The Wiser,
rolling her eyes. "But we had a meeting,
and decided that we really, **REALLY,
REALLY** wanted to do it, and

you can't want something more than that. Unless you really, **REALLY, REALLY, REALLY** want it.* Suffice to say we couldn't think of anything we wanted more. We put it to a vote and everything. So three sacrifices to the Loch Less Monster it is."

"Wait," I said, trying hard not to smile in case it gave the game away. "Your plan is to sacrifice us to the Loch Less Monster?"

"Isn't that what I said?"

"Please, no, not the Loch Less Monster," I sobbed, doing my best to sound as if I truly meant it. "Anything but that!"

Nun The Wiser stared at me with a look of pity, as if she'd expected better.

"Have you quite finished?" she said.

"For the moment," I said, "but I may sob some more when the sacrifice begins."

"Good. Because I couldn't help thinking for a second there that you were only pretending to be scared because you thought we meant to sacrifice you to Lessie."

* And that, as I mentioned earlier, would be extremely silly.

I was baffled.

Bewildered.

Some might even say befuddled.

"Is that NOT what you intend to do?" I said.

"Why would we do that?" laughed Nun The Wiser. "She's harmless. Between you and me, Jack, I've even started to suspect she might be a submarine. No, we're sacrificing you to the REAL Loch Less Monster."

Nun The Wiser spun round to face the water.

It was broiling and foaming, as if the cold soup it resembled was heating up on a stove at last. Remembering how Dad's stew had erupted, I watched the commotion uneasily.

Near to shore, there was a plash . . . then a splash . . . then a splosh . . . and a sploosh.

There was even a kersploosh.

A head emerged from the water.

A dark head with flaming eyes and smoke billowing from its nostrils.

It was the Noggle.

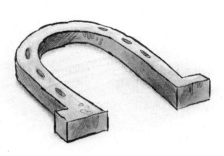

# The Last
# Chapter
# Ever

If I could have untied my hands and held the monster hunting manual one last time, the title on the front would have said: *Monster Hunting For Boys Who Know The End Is Nigh*.

I'd seen the entry on Noggles last night. There was no reasoning with them.

This one was going to drag us down to its lair under the water and devour us, and there was nothing we could do to stop it.

Step by step it advanced towards us, that nasty, hobnailed bridle with its metal chains for reins still fastened to its head, eyes growing more fiery and the smoke from its nostrils more billowy as it drew nearer.

The Noggle came to a halt with its face inches

from mine. I felt its hot breath on my skin as its mouth opened wide.

The smell of smoke made me want to choke. Its smouldering eyes drilled into me.

This was going to be the shortest chapter in either of my adventures so far. It was also going to be the last one ever. I screwed my eyes shut, hoping that it would at least eat me quickly rather than taking its time between mouthfuls so that people didn't think it was greedy.

Goodbye, cruel world!

# The Last Chapter After the Last Chapter Ever

I wasn't dead yet.

That was usually a **Hopeful Sign**.

I opened my eyes the tiniest crack.

The Noggle was still there, staring into my eyes with a strange expression.

"What's going on?" cried Nun The Wiser, outraged that I hadn't been devoured yet.

"No idea," I said. "But I'll be sure to let you know the minute I find out."

It seemed that I'd spoken too soon. The

Noggle's mouth was opening again.

Was I going to be eaten anyway, only more slowly than I'd hoped a few moments ago?

A long, rough tongue emerged from the Noggle's lips . . . and licked my face from chin to eyebrows and all points in between.

The sensation was a bit too sticky for my liking, but it was better than teeth.

I was almost afraid to open my mouth in case I got an unwanted taste of Noggle spit.

"Mgghmmmfffbbbmmmgg?" I mumbled between licks of the Noggle's tongue.

Luckily, Nancy understood – or guessed – what I was trying to ask her.

"It recognises you," she said. "You're the boy who gave it your last sausage roll. The Noggle couldn't eat YOU."

As if to prove it, the Noggle licked me again, the chainlike reins on its bridle jangling all the while. This time its tongue went up my nose.

That must have been even more unpleasant for the Noggle than it was for me.*

* I was wrong. I've since learned that there's nothing a Noggle likes better than the taste of fresh bogey.

"Noggle," I said, "could you kindly bite through our chains and set us free?"

What I actually said was "Gggmmmhmmmfffmmmggbbb," but the Noggle seemed to understand me too.

The horse reached its head behind the pole to where my hands were fastened, and snapped through the metal links as if they were no harder than onion rings.

In seconds, I was free. It did the same for Nancy, and Nun The Less.

"I must admit, I didn't expect this **Unexpected Twist**," Nun The Wiser declared. "That must be why they call them unexpected. I thought we'd be back at the Abbey enjoying a hearty post-sacrifice fry up by now."

Nancy and I threw our arms round the Noggle's neck in thanks for saving us, but it flinched at the touch, as if in pain.

"Look," I noticed. "The bridle's so tight it's digging into the poor thing's skin."

"I wonder," said Nancy, who often did.

"What do you wonder?" I asked.

"What I wonder," she said, "is whether Monster Hunting for Beginners is wrong. It wouldn't be the first time."

"You mean . . .?"

"Yes, that's exactly what I mean," said Nancy. "At least, it is if what you mean is that you don't gain control of a Noggle by stealing its bridle, but by putting a bridle ON it in the first place. Wild horses aren't meant to wear bridles! What if that's what's hurting the poor thing?"

"Let's take it off and see," I said.

Nun The Less stepped up to give a hand.

Ignoring the shouts of the nuns who pleaded with us not to take the bridle off, we managed to loosen it and lift it free of the Noggle's head.

The bridle was so heavy, it took all three of us together to set it down on the ground.

How had the Noggle not sunk to the bottom of Loch Less under that awful weight?

At once the horse put back its head and whinnied happily, before running round in circles and coming back to lick us both again.

"Hffmmmggmmbbbmmgg," said Nancy, learning what it was like to get her own face washed by a Noggle's wet tongue.

I guessed what she was saying too.

It was: "Who could be so wicked as to put a nice Noggle under their **Sinister Influence**?"

"I can think of a few someones who would," I said, turning to the Sisters of Perpetual Misery with a look that said they'd better start explaining themselves fast or they'd have us to contend with.

# Still Not the Last Chapter

"Congratulations. I suppose," said Nun The Wiser, giving Nancy and me a slow hand clap.

"You figured out our **Vile Scheme**."

"Not all of it," I said. "We still don't know why you've been tormenting this innocent Noggle."

"We needed a place to live," she explained. "Nun The Worse read in some old tale that Noggles were best for the job, so she made a bridle from her own design,* hid by Loch Less one night as the Noggle came out of the loch to graze, and threw it over him like you do when

---

* That accounted for all the hobnails.

you toss a ring over a toy to win it at the fairground. After that, he was in our power, and had no choice but to build us an abbey."

"How did he build anything when he only has hooves?" said Nancy, ever the one for spotting impracticalities.

"How should I know?" said Nun The Wiser with a shrug. "Let's say he used some special abbey-building magic Noggles have."

"You can't use magic as an excuse every time you don't understand something," Nancy said disapprovingly.

"Then maybe he has lots of gnome builders on the workforce who do it for him," said Nun The Wiser. "What matters is there was a lot of hammering and sawing and banging through the night, and the next day there stood Muckle Abbey. But there was a catch."

"There usually is," I agreed.

"On the first anniversary of the construction of the abbey, Nun The Worse said we had to offer a sacrifice to the Noggle in payment. That was in the old tales too. We didn't think too much of it at the time. A year seemed a long way off. Recently we realised the day was near and decided you'd make the perfect sacrifice. It would be killing two birds with one stone. We wanted to punish you for what you'd done to Nun The Worse, and the Noggle needed a victim. So we wrote asking for help in the hope you'd come. To be honest, I'm surprised you fell for it, Jack. Lubbers aren't dangerous. They're merely a nuisance. Like fleas. Getting rid of them is fleasy peasy."*

"Does this mean the Noggle still needs a victim?" I said, though it seemed highly unlikely as I watched it rolling around in the flowers like an excitable pup and scratching its itchy backside on a tree stump.

"If you're thinking of sacrificing me to the Noggle," said Nun The Wiser, "forget it."

---

*I could almost hear Stoop's voice in my head saying: "What did I tell you?"*

"Why not?" I said with a grin. "You were going to sacrifice us."

"That was different. We're wicked, and you're not. You wouldn't have the guts to go through with it. Besides, there are still far more of US than there are of YOU."

Behind Nun The Wiser, I saw the Sisters of Perpetual Misery lined up ready for a scrap.

# Ready
# Or Not

Maths had never been my strongest subject in
school, as I may have previously mentioned.
But even I could see we were outnumbered.

Quickly, I did a head count to see how our
opposing forces measured up.

On our side was me, Nancy, Nun The Less,
and the Noggle. That made four.*

Facing us was Nun The Wiser . . . Second To
Nun . . . Nun Whatsoever . . . Nun Of This . . .
Nun Of That . . . Nun Too Soon . . . Nun Left . . .
Nun Of The Above . . .

I gave up as I ran out of fingers.

There were LOTS of nuns, and only one of
them was on our side.**

* Even I could work out that sum.
** That was Nun The Less, in case of confusion.

"Surrender immediately, and we might go easy on you," Nun The Wiser offered. "But we probably won't because we are quite bad."

"Never!" we swore.* "It's you who should surrender to us. We're coming, ready or not."

"You and whose army?" she said.

"Bill's army!" came a voice I knew well.

Down the road from the direction of Muckle Abbey marched a troop of Lubbers with Bill at their head, all ready to make good on Bill's promise to come to our aid if we were ever in a tight spot. Soon there were Bills here, and Bills there, and Bills everywhere.**

"Oh," said Nun The Wiser. "You DO have an army. That's a bit of a nuisance."

"Two of them, actually," announced a second and equally welcome voice.

Glancing towards the shore, I saw Borborygmus, Most Gaseous Ruler of the **Loch Creatures**, leading her people out of the murky depths and on to land.

They were wearing their own diving suits, with

* *I mean that we made a solemn promise, not that we used bad words.*
** *Just like the Sisters of Perpetual Misery's first message said, more or less.*

242

tubes leading from the tops of their heads back into the loch, to keep them supplied with water to breathe, and they were carrying spears made from the long jawbones of fish.

"We have resolved to hide no longer, **Great One**!" burbled Borborygmus inside her helmet as she advanced up the slope.

"**Great One**?" inquired Nancy, raising an eyebrow.

"It's a long story," I said awkwardly.

The Loch Creatures duly joined our ranks, introducing themselves politely to the Lubbers, and the Lubbers did the same to them.*

The Lubbers were particularly taken with the liquidy bubbling noises that issued regularly from the seats of the **Loch Creatures**' diving suits, and attempted – with great success – to produce the same effect in the air.

"Your two armies hold no fear for us," maintained Nun The Wiser, but there was a new doubt in her voice.

"What about three armies?" said Nancy,

* It was a lot easier to remember the Lubbers' names than the Loch Creatures'.

pointing a finger into the distance.

Out on the water, the *Great Haul* sailed into view, one famous smuggler at the wheel, followed by an enormous shifting cloud of fog.

"I asked Rochester to fetch the Fog Goblins last night when we found out you had Jack in your clutches," Nancy told Nun The Wiser. "I thought their skills might come in handy."

In an instant, visibility was down to a few feet and the smell of porridge filled the air as the Fog Goblins swirled about with their pig-like nostrils and distorted grins, eager to help their new friend Nancy in her hour of need.

"We're not afraid of a bit of fog," said Nun The Wiser, as the Sisters of Perpetual Misery reached as one into their robes and produced the needle-sharp swords they'd been concealing there all along.

That was their biggest mistake.

# Fight!

Nun The Wiser was first to be picked up.

The Fog Goblins lifted her by the ankle, before whirling her round and round to build up momentum, and then flinging her at vast speed into the distance where the thick, clammy, porridgey air swallowed her up.

A new game of Hoo-Shank had begun.

The Sisters of Perpetual Misery rushed to rescue Nun The Wiser as hastily as their clumsy hobnail boots could allow, but they were no match for Fog Goblins.

One by one, the nuns were hoisted off the ground in the same way and tossed back and forth like bean bags. I couldn't help feeling a bit sorry for them. I knew what it was like.

Whenever one of them managed to wriggle

out of the Fog Goblins' grasp for a second and try to make their way to safety, the Loch Creatures darted forward and jabbed them on the bottom with their fishbone spears.

Leaping into the air to escape the sharp tips, the nuns were promptly picked up again for another round of Hoo-Shank.

The Lubbers were less effective in a scrap, but they were having a jolly time of it all the same as they galloped round in circles, giggling giddily at the satisfying sight of the nuns getting their comeuppance.

Rochester was kept busiest of all, fishing out the nuns who landed in the water, before depositing them soggily back on shore, where they were promptly grabbed again by the Fog Goblins for another round of Hoo-Shank.

"Do you give up?" I yelled at Nun The Wiser as she whizzed past.

"Yeeeeeeeeeeeeessssss!"

"Do you promise never to capture Noggles again?"

"Weeeeeeedddddddddooooooo!"

"And not to torment poor Lubbers and ghosts?"

"Ifyoooouinsssiiiiiiisssssstt!"

That was good enough for Nancy.

"Fog Goblins, desist!" she ordered.

The nuns fluttered down to earth like bedraggled blackbirds, collapsing on to the grass and lying still to cure their dizziness.*

Last and dizziest of the lot, Nun The Wiser was deposited heavily in their midst.

Never had the Sisters of Perpetual Misery looked so miserable.

Their work done, the Fog Goblins dispersed, taking the smell of porridge with them, and calm returned to Loch Less.

"We are defeated at last," said Nun The Wiser when she could tell her ups from her downs and her lefts from rights once more. "Out with it, Jack! What dire but deserved punishment do you have in store for us?"

* Being the projectiles in a game of Hoo Shank isn't good for the nerves.

"I'm not big into punishing, to be honest,"
I said. "I wouldn't know where to begin. Why
don't you go back to Muckle Abbey and we'll
pretend this whole thing never happened?"

"We can't," said Nun The Wiser mournfully.
"The year is up. No sacrifice was made. The
magic the Noggle used to build it has run out.
That means Muckle Abbey will . . ."

"Collapse!" screeched the nuns.

A nearby crash confirmed the worst.

Muckle Abbey teetered and tottered and
toppled in on itself like a cake that's been taken
out of the oven too early.

It wasn't until the nuns' **GINORMOUS**
former home had been reduced to nothing but a
**MIDDLING** heap of stones that I remembered
there'd still been one **LITTLE** man inside when
it fell down.

# Rise and Shine

Nancy and I made it to the **Scene Of Destruction** in double quick time. It may even have been triple quick time. Neither of us had a speedometer on hand to check.

All we cared about was finding out if Stoop had woken up and got to safety before the walls and roof of Muckle Abbey caved in.

The sight that greeted us was **Not Encouraging**.

The only thing to survive the demolition was the table at which we* had eaten earlier. It sat on its own among the ruins like a loyal guard dog who hasn't noticed yet that there's nothing left to guard.

Stoop was sitting in the exact same chair, head slumped forward in a bowl of cabbage.

* *By which I mean Stoop.*

I clambered over the fallen debris and shook his shoulder gently, not knowing what I would do if he'd **Breathed His Last**.

For a moment it seemed he had.

Then abruptly his body jerked, as if someone had attached electrodes to each side of his head and turned on the power supply, which I promise I hadn't.**

Stoop sat up straight, no longer green, yawning and stretching his arms before gaping at me in **Momentary Confusion**.

"I must have nodded off," he said still sleepily. "Did I miss anything?"

"No, Stoop," I said in delight as he picked a piece of dusty cabbage out of his beard and bit into it. "You didn't miss a thing."

"Needs more salt," he grumbled, helping himself to another morsel.

"I don't understand," I said as the Sisters of Perpetual Misery, prevented from getting here quicker by their hobnail boots, stepped

** *I wouldn't know how..*

into the wreckage of their former home. "The Noggle's not bad. It can't be to blame for this."

The Noggle whinnied as if to say, "I should think not."

"Then what destroyed the abbey?" asked Nun The Less.

"Not what," said Nancy. "Who."

I sniffed the air.

I knew that smell.

"Hatfield," I said.

# Cough Up

I didn't mean that Hatfield was smelly.

There were many unpleasant things about the owner* of Monster Management Solutions, but his armpits weren't one of them.

What I'd smelled was bananas, marzipan and fart, as in Nun Of The Above's room after Nancy blasted a hole in the wall,** but the aroma was much stronger because Hatfield had used his entire supply of dynamite to blow Muckle Abbey to smithereens.

Up from the rubble rose the man himself.

His hair was charred, and what was left of his eyebrows after the earlier incident with the fireworks had been shot clean off.

Otherwise he was in tip-top condition for someone who'd undergone a close encounter

* And now sole employee again.
** Together with the other smell, but I really do think we should try to forget about that completely.

with high explosives seconds ago.

"What did you do that for?" I shouted. "You might have killed someone!"

"Don't blame me!" said Hatfield, tugging rubble from his ears. "I didn't expect the explosion to be so destructive. Then someone let out the BIGGEST blast of gas from his nether regions, right as the dynamite was about to go off, and . . . kapow . . . everything went up in smoke!"

"Sorry about that," said Stoop. "I had eaten an enormous amount of cabbage. All that fart power has to go somewhere, even when I am asleep."

(He wasn't kidding. At home I was often woken by the sound of thunder in the night, only to realise that the rumbling was actually coming from the shed at the bottom of the garden.)

"But why did you want to blow up Muckle Abbey at all?" I said, still baffled.

"Haven't you guessed?" Nancy pronounced. "It was Hatfield who set this whole brilliant – if over-complicated – plan into motion."

"It's true," said Hatfield. "I once had to spend a night in hospital after hearing the nuns sing. I knew if they held their choir practice outside Mop and Mow's house that the ghosts would be driven out. And if they could then be persuaded to move into the castle, the Lubbers would be scared off and need a new place of their own to live – and where better than under the flagstones of Muckle Abbey?"

I knew what was coming next.

"Yes, Jack, I am the Mysterious Stranger!"

Hatfield gave an **Evil Laugh**, but he wasn't very good at it. It sounded more like a quack, as if he was doing an impression of a duck.*

"It had to be Hatfield," Nancy said. "He's the only one we met since arriving in Muckle who even has a hood. Which is odd, when you think about it, because it does rain a lot."

* A duck who was no good at Evil Laughs either.

Stoop declared he could kick himself for not figuring it out. He then proceeded to do it hard, once on each shin with the opposite foot.

"That does tie up a few loose ends," I said. "But it still doesn't explain why you destroyed Muckle Abbey. "

"For revenge, what else?" answered Hatfield. "I only became the Mysterious Stranger because the Sisters of Perpetual Misery hired me to lure you to Muckle Abbey in time for the sacrifice. I kept my end of the bargain, but when I presented Nun The Wiser with the bill for my services*, she refused to cough up. No, I tell a lie, she DID cough up. All over me. It was disgusting. But she wouldn't hand over a penny. That's when I resolved to get my own back on them by blowing up their home. I'm not like Poop. I can't work for job satisfaction alone."

Stoop muttered that he'd be getting some job satisfaction from sticking Hatfield's head in a mountain of Fuddy-Duddy dung if he didn't start saying his name properly.

* He meant a demand for money, not a Bill like one of the Lubbers.

"But I told you at the start that we had no money," Nun The Wiser said to Hatfield. "You said you were happy to do it for free publicity for your new business."

"I changed my mind," he said. "Gnashers this white don't come cheap, you know."

Hatfield tried flashing one of his famous smiles, but his teeth were now black with soot. Some of them were missing. The blast had blown them right out of his mouth.

Everyone laughed as he began scrambling through the rubble in search of them.

"I suppose, all things considered, we got what we deserved," said Nun The Wiser, "but we have paid a **Dreadful Price**."

And she pointed into the wreckage at a giant pair of hobnail boots made of stone.

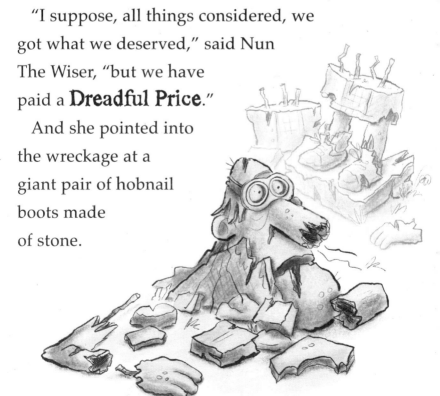

# Hot Cross Nuns

"Nun The Worse is no more," said Nun The Wiser sorrowfully, bowing her head.

"I never liked her anyway," muttered a rebellious voice from among the other nuns.

"What did you say, Second To Nun?" said Nun The Wiser hotly.

"I said I didn't like her, and I mean it," said Nun The Less hotter still.

"I hated her too," joined in Nun Other, hottest of all, "but I was afraid to say it out loud. Nun The Worse was **MEAN**. She once made me stand on my head for a week when she caught me smiling without permission."*

* *I can confirm that this was indeed the sort of thing Aunt Prudence liked to do.*

"Well, we ARE the Sisters of Perpetual Misery," pointed out Nun The Wiser, "not the Sisters of Incessant Jollity."

"Incessant means never-ending too," Nancy whispered to me helpfully again.

"I know!" I said.*

"I don't care what we're called," said Nun Of The Above, so hotly that her eyebrows started smouldering. "I never even liked being a nun."

"Nor did I," said Nun Too Soon. "It was boring, and these hobnail boots are so uncomfortable. I wish we had some pink, fluffy slippers like Nun The Less."

"I always dreamed of being an explorer," chipped in Nun Too Pleased.

"I want to be a racing driver," said Nun At All.

"We've been secretly making plans to run away and open a stray cats' home," said Nun Of This and Nun Of That.

"Can I come and work there too?" said

* *I still didn't really.*

Second To Nun.

"You'd be more than welcome."

"I'm sure you can all guess what I want to be," said the nun who'd been dressed as a traffic warden when we arrived.

She tore off her robe to reveal she was still wearing her favourite uniform underneath.

Nun Of Your Business, needless to say, refused to reveal her plans for the future.

"I quite enjoyed being a nun to begin with," Nun The Less admitted in a quiet voice when everyone else had finished having their say. "You know, before Nun The Worse started bossing us about to be wicked."

Nun The Wiser smiled at Nun The Less.

"Why don't you and I stop being enemies and set up a new order of our own?" she said.

"A not-evil one?"

"If you absolutely insist."

"I do," said Nun The Less. "But can we please call it something more cheerful? I'm fed up of

Perpetual Misery."

"It's a deal," said Nun The Wiser.

"Count me in too," proclaimed Rochester, who'd finally found a place to moor the *Great Haul*, before trekking up the headland to see what was going on. "Those outfits you've got on are the perfect disguise for my line of work. Who'd suspect a nun of being a smuggler?"

"To tell the truth," said Nun The Wiser, "I wasn't very fond of Nun The Worse either. I had loads of sleepless nights feeling guilty about what she'd done to the poor Noggle. My doctor said it was the lack of sleep that was making me so wicked."

"If you're all done planning the rest of your lives," said Nancy, "I think you'll find there's something you've overlooked."

"What is it?"

"The prophecy, remember?" Nancy said.

"What prophecy?" said Hatfield, trying to insert tiny white stones into his blackened gums in the hope they'd look like teeth.

"Didn't the Sisters of Perpetual Misery tell you?" said Nancy. "Muckle Abbey sits on an entrance to the **Underworld**. Should it ever fall down, the creatures who live there would be free to crawl and slither out and, before you know it, it'd be **THE END OF THE WORLD AS WE KNOW IT!**"

"Don't panic," said Nun The Wiser. "That was just something Nun The Worse made up to give us nightmares. We only told you about it so that you'd **Do Our Bidding**."

"If Aunt Prudence made it up," I gulped, "what's that **Ominous Rumbling** under our feet?"

# Monsters Galore

Soon it was as if we were standing on the lid of a huge pot that was shaking as it came to the boil. Something even worse than Dad's stew was bound to shoot out when it did.

Cracks appeared in the ground.

Through them, we saw fire and lava bubbling deep below. An awful stench filled the air. It smelled like rotten eggs. Not just any old rotten eggs, but rotten eggs that are so rotten even the other rotten eggs don't want to sit next to them on account of the smell.

Flames curled up from the cracks, flicking round our feet like a Noggle's tongue.

It was hot, like when you open the oven door as dinner's roasting and your glasses instantly steam up. My glasses were misting over now, and it would have been a relief if they'd stayed that way because I wouldn't have seen what was rising from the ground.

Peeking through my fingers, I saw **Haggles** and **Puckles** . . . **Skullduggers** . . . **Malarkeys** and **Collywobbles**.

All the **Underworld** monsters I'd read about in my book last night were pulling themselves up out of the hot mud with a sucking sound.

There were even **Flittertigibbets**.

# Flittertigibbets

*Flittertigibbets were once best known for stealing children before realising that they didn't like them. They always brought them home after a few days, whether their parents wanted them back or not. And they often didn't, having realised that they could make extra money renting out their children's bedrooms to people who needed a place to sleep and didn't mind stepping over all the usual mess there is lying about children's bedrooms to get to bed.*

The monsters shuffled and slithered towards us, some on webbed feet, some on pads, some on misshapen toes, wrenching open their mouths wide to whine and whisper and yowl and shriek, as well as making other noises too unspeakable to put into words.*

At the head of the pack was a huge, bull-like **Malarkey**, its steel horns glowing redly from the fire from which it had crawled.

"This is your chance to redeem yourself," I said to Hatfield. "Stay and fight this terrible army alongside us and prove yourself worthy of the title of monster hunter."

For a moment, I thought Hatfield might do it. Then he looked over and saw one of the **Collywobbles** slithering towards him. It was even uglier and more terrifying than the picture

---

* *That's what made them unspeakable, because that's what unspeakable means.*

in *Monster Hunting for Beginners*.

"Not ruddy likely!" he yelled.

He dropped his stone teeth, turned on his heels, and fled in the opposite direction.

He wasn't much of a monster hunter, but he could run quite fast, I'll give him that.

The rest of us got ready to fight.

Nancy and I climbed on to the friendly Noggle's back. I took out my catapult, and passed Nancy the wooden sword.*

Stoop unhooked as many weapons from his belt as he could hold at once without risking an accident, because this wasn't the moment to stop and rummage through his bag for a plaster if anyone cut their finger.

"I'll save Muckle from these foul brutes if it kills me," he muttered, before adding, "and it probably will."

Rochester joined us, pulling a pair of pistols from the inside pockets of her long coat, whilst the nuns drew their needle-sharp

---

* *This was not the time to worry about that old Not Hurting Monsters rule.*

blades and prepared for
battle a second time, only now
we were all on the same side.

Even the **Lubbers** and the **Loch Creatures**
stood their ground, which was brave of them,
because I wouldn't have blamed anyone for
running away.*

"Let battle begin!" roared the **Malarkey**.
And battle did.

* *Except Hatfield.*

# Our Luck Runs Out

I'd like to say that it was a mighty clash that would go down in monster hunting history and be talked about for centuries to come.

That would be a lie.

The fight was over in about three minutes.

Four and a half, at the most.

I managed to hit a couple of monsters with rocks from my catapult, but the stones bounced off their skin like rain off a tin roof.

Nancy's sword burned down to the hilt on the very first **Puckle** that she struck, because the monster was still sizzling hot from being in the **Fiery Pits of Doom** for so long.

The nuns' swords were equally useless.

They all snapped, or bent on contact with the enemy, while Snoop was sat on heavily by a Haggle approximately seven seconds in and couldn't move for the rest of the battle.

The **Lubbers** and **Loch Creatures** did their best, but fighting wasn't their speciality.

Soon we were all caught and held tight by various arms and flippers and tentacles.

The **Collywobbles** took charge of Nancy and Rochester. The **Puckles** clung on tight to the slippery **Lubbers**. The **Flittertigibbets** tied up the **Noggle** with the tube connecting **Borborygmus's** helmet to the water tank on her back, keeping them both under control, and her fellow **Loch Creatures** were rounded up easily by the remaining **Skullduggers**.

For my part, I was almost overcome by the stink of dog food and sour milk as the **Malarkey** nabbed me from behind.

"You don't scare us," mumbled Stoop from under the **Haggle**, though I have to admit he was mistaken about that.

Getting killed now and again might be an **Occupational Hazard** for a professional monster hunter,* but we didn't have to like it.

At that moment, I didn't like it one bit.

"I'm more worried what's going to happen AFTER they've killed us," said Nancy.

"There IS something we have to do after killing you, now you mention it," said the **Malarkey**, "but I've clean forgotten what it is."

One of the **Skullduggers** came forward and whispered something in its ear. Or the hole in the side of its head where the ear would be if it had any.

"That's right," the **Malarkey** growled. "Silly me. Apparently, it's all written down in some ancient prophecy. Not that we've seen it. We're only going on what we were told by Nun The Worse. She was always popping in and out of the **Underworld** to remind us to get ready for the end of the world as we know it."

"Why does no one say it right?" said Nancy.

---

* *That means it's something we have to be prepared for in the course of a day's work.*

274

"It's **THE END OF THE WORLD AS WE KNOW IT**."

"Does it really matter at this stage?" I said.

"It's always important to get the details right," Nancy insisted.

"Just do one favour for me," Stoop said to the monster under whose monstrous bottom he was currently squashed. "Let Crabbit know I tried to save Muckle – and the rest of the world too, if at all possible, but mainly Muckle. I want him to be proud of me."

"Since you asked so nicely, I'll do it," the Haggle vowed. "Right before I kill him too."

"You're a gentleman," said Stoop.

So that was that. Our luck was out. This time it really was over. We'd be gobbled up. The world would end. I'd never get the chance to write a third book of my adventures.

And that's what probably would have happened had a sound I knew only too well not suddenly reached my ears.

# Who's Afraid of Oooooooohs?

"Oooooooooooh!"

"Ooooooooohh!"

I'd have recognised those voices anywhere. There were only two souls who could **Oooooooooooh** like that.

Mop and Mow had managed to exchange their plain ghostly tablecloths for a pair of nice patterned ones and were now wafting up to the ruins of Muckle Abbey, taking it in turns to **Ooooooooh** at the assembled monsters.

I was touched that they wanted to help, but I couldn't see what two ghosts could do against a whole army of monsters from the deepest depths of the **Underworld**.

Then I felt the **Malarkey** who was holding on to me start to shake.

"You're not afraid of a couple of ghosts, are you?" I said, almost laughing.

"They ARE ghosts then?" the **Malarkey** said. "I hoped I was imagining them."

"They're ghosts all right," I said, realising that this might be a chance to **Turn The Tables**. "They're two of the most ghastly ghosts that ever haunted Muckle. Scerrifying, they are."

The Malarkey shuddered some more.

"They're not the only ghosts either," said Nancy. "We're ghosts too, aren't we, Jack?"

"Are we?" I said, confused.

"Of course we are. Don't you remember?"

Nancy put back her head and let out a great "**Oooooooooooooh**!" of her own.

I saw her plan, and began **Oooooooohing** as well. I still didn't have the hang of it like she

did, but it was enough to set the other
monsters shaking and shuddering.

"That sound!" they began crying, letting go
of their captives so they could cover their ears.*

"Stop! We can't bear it!"

"It's making our blood run cold,
and we don't even have any," said
the **Haggles**.

"It's making our flesh creep,"
said the **Puckles**, "and we don't
have any either."

"Yes, you do, it's all over your bodies,"
pointed out the Lubbers. "Well, mostly. There
are a few patches missing, true enough."

We were all free now, including Stoop,
but the monsters were still dangerous while
they were up here on the surface rather
than down in the
**Underworld**

* *If they had any.*

where they belonged.

Effective as they were, the **Ooooooohs** wouldn't be enough. We needed more ammunition.

"Quick!" I said to the nuns. "Sing!"

Nun The Wiser understood what I was getting at. Immediately, she gathered the Sisters of Perpetual Misery in a circle to begin their last ever choir practice.

The noise was horrendous. If they hadn't been on our side, I would have surrendered at once to get them to stop.

It had the same effect on the rest of the **Haggles**, **Puckles**, **Skullduggers**, **Flittergibbets** and **Collywobbles**. As one they screamed and dived headfirst into the flaming crack.

The Malarkey pitched in

last of all.

The ground closed up after them with a noise like the smacking of wet lips.

"Well done! You saved the world from ending," cried Nancy to Mop and Mow, as the Lubbers danced with excitement around and even through them, no longer afraid of ghosts.

"Look, Mop," said Mow, "it's those funny chaps we saw at the castle."

"So it is," said Mop. "Aren't they sweet?"

They were all soon the best of friends.

"What a way to end another adventure," I remarked to Nancy as the two ghosts and the Lubbers wandered off together back to their own homes, making plans to meet up again regularly to have **Ooooooohing** competitions. "The story's not over yet," said Stoop gruffly. "There's still one monster left."

# Nigel the Great

I didn't recognise this particular monster from the **Underworld** section of *Monster Hunting for Beginners*, but that might have been because it was dressed up as if for a holiday.

It was wearing sunglasses and sandals and baggy shorts and a brightly patterned Hawaiian shirt. On its head was a baseball cap with a plastic propeller on top that spun round when a breeze blew. This monster was even holding a suitcase with a sticker stuck to the side that said **I'm Only Here For The Fear**.

It looked as if it had been . . . on holiday?

"Who are you?" I asked carefully, because you never know what you're dealing with when a new monster comes along. It could have

---

* *That's a False Sense Of Security, in case you've forgotten.*

been trying to lull us into a FSOS.*

"I'm Nigel," the monster said.

"Nigel?" I repeated, because that didn't sound like a very monstrous name.*

"Yes, Nigel. With an N."

"Is there any other kind of Nigel?" asked Stoop, but the monster said it wasn't an expert on Nigels so couldn't say for sure.

"If you'd rather call me something else," it went on, "I'm also known at home as the **Considerably-Sized Beast of Muckle Moor**."

"You're real, after all!" I exclaimed.

"I was last time I checked," the **Considerably-Sized Beast** said uncertainly. "I haven't been around for a while. It gets very cold up on the moor, what with all the fog, so I thought I'd go on a wee trip down into the **Underworld**, because I'd heard it was lovely and warm down there. And it is. I had a smashing time, until I tried to come back home, and discovered that someone had plonked a

---

* Mainly because it isn't.

great big abbey on top of the entrance."

"I do apologise," said Nun The Wiser. "That was our fault. Though in our defence, we didn't know the **Considerably-Sized Beast of Muckle Moor** was real either, so it never occurred to us that you'd need a door."

"I forgive you. I should have checked there was another way out before going in," Nigel said. "You have no idea how glad I am to be back out again in the fresh air. There's only so much heat a **Considerably-Sized Beast** can take before it gets too much. It's so good to see Loch Less again."

**The Beast** took off its sunglasses to get a better look at the water.

It was then that I noticed it had three eyes – one on the left and one on the right in the usual arrangement, with an extra one in the middle.

I gasped.

When it took off the cap, I gasped again as two ears fell out, flopping down on either side of its bald head like a basset hound's.

"Borborygmus," I said, turning to the **Loch Creatures**, who were still trying to untangle their leader from the Noggle. "Did you bring your picture of the **Great One**?"

"We did indeed, **Reluctant Great One**," said their **Most Gaseous Ruler**. "We never leave home without it. Why do you ask?"

"Because I think I've found the REAL **Great One**," I said, presenting her with the **Considerably-Sized Beast of Muckle Moor**.

The **Loch Creatures** checked the new monster's appearance against the portrait from the ancient scrolls. There was no denying it.

"**Great One**, it's you!" they cried, bowing down low, and begging the **Beast** to come to the secret underwater city and be their leader.

"Joint leader really," clarified Borborygmus. "I've decided I quite like being a **Most Gaseous Ruler**, but I'm prepared to share power. We can rule on alternate days, taking

Sundays off so the **Loch Creatures** get a break from being bossed about. What do you say?"

"Don't mind if I do," said Nigel.

It picked up its suitcase, and was led off to begin a new life, just as soon as it could be fitted with a considerably-sized diving suit.

I grinned. Everyone could now go back where they belonged, not least the Noggle who could live peacefully in Loch Less without being compelled to wear a bridle or build anything ever again unless it really wanted to.

Nun The Wiser, Nun The Less and Rochester were even eagerly discussing their plans to construct a new abbey on top of the **Underworld** to keep the monsters who lurked down there from getting out in future.*

There was only one more thing we had to do before the adventure was over.

* Rochester said they could live on her boat in the meantime.

# Catching Up

"Stoop, my boy!" said Crabbit when he answered the knock at Dunmoanin to see his long lost son standing on the doorstep for the first time in two hundred years. "How've you been?"

"Mustn't grumble," said Stoop.* "Keeping busy, you know."

"You have done well for yourself, I must say," Crabbit said, leading Stoop inside and insisting he sit in the best chair nearest the fire. "I've read all about you in *Monster Hunting News*. I have it delivered every week to see what you're up to. I've kept all the cuttings."

"You're not still annoyed that I became a monster hunter then?" said Stoop in surprise.

"I never objected to you hunting monsters,"

*In truth he did little else.

insisted Crabbit. "I just wanted you to wait until you were a bit older before setting out into the world on your own. You were only seven years old. It's a father's job to protect his children, and you were so small back then. But look how you've grown. You're huge!"

Stoop blushed. "Do you really think so?"

"Why, you're taller than Uncle Carnaptious, and he's practically a giant to the rest of us."

Stoop blushed even deeper.

Was that a little tear in his eye?

Looking away so that we didn't embarrass him, Nancy and I gazed round at all the pictures of Stoop that covered the wall.

There was one of him as a baby in his cot, clutching a bottle and a fluffy monster toy, but looking exactly the same, complete with red nose and beard. Another showed him on his first* day at school. He wore a baggy uniform and a cap, and was scowling at the camera on account of being asked to smile.**

It wasn't hard to see why everyone had

---

* And only.
** How they'd taken photographs years before cameras were invented wasn't explained.

recognised him after two hundred years away.

He hadn't changed a bit.

It was funny* to realise the grumpy monster hunter who'd taken me on as his apprentice had once been young like us, dreaming of adventure, not knowing if he'd ever find it.

It was even more funny** to see him now, perched shyly on an armchair with his legs sticking out, drinking tea and being loaded with cupcakes topped with dollops of icing sugar.***

Crabbit said he made them specially every year on Stoop's birthday, on the off chance that his son would pop in for a visit.

"Nancy and I didn't know today was your birthday, Stoop," I said.

"Nor did I," said Stoop.

"Then tonight we'll make up for lost time," said Crabbit, heading to the kitchen to bake more cupcakes because he was down to the last three dozen and they wouldn't last longer

* Peculiar, not haha.
** Haha, not peculiar.
*** They'd always been his favourite treat, it seemed.

than three more pots of tea at the most.

"Does this mean we owe you two hundred presents for all the ones you missed?" I asked.

"I'm not an unreasonable man," Stoop said. "I'll settle for a hundred and ninety-nine. In fact, Nancy, I have a gift for you."

"For me?" Nancy said in astonishment, because Stoop had never given her anything before, except for a sore wrist from beating him so often at those arm wrestling contests.

Stoop reached into his bag and pulled out a copy of *Monster Hunting For Beginners* specially for her. But it wasn't called that.

When she touched it, the title on the front cover changed to *Monster Hunting For Clever And Intrepid Girls Called Nancy.**

"I thought you said I wasn't a proper apprentice monster hunter?" she said.

"You proved me wrong," he said. "Jack and I would have been at the mercy of those nuns if you hadn't ridden to the rescue."

* Intrepid means fearless and adventurous, which summed up Nancy to a tee.

He was awkwardly trying to stop Nancy hugging him when Crabbit came back from the kitchen, complaining that he needed a bigger oven. He'd only managed to fit in another thirteen trays of cupcakes.

It was remarkable how much he looked like his son, except that Crabbit's nose was slightly redder and his beard a good deal shaggier.

It was only when I saw his coat hanging on a hook behind the door that I realised.

"It was you," I said, "standing in the rain outside The Smuggler's Inn that first night."

"Guilty as charged," Crabbit said. "I'd heard that Stoop was back in town. Word gets round fast in a place like Muckle. I was considering throwing a stone at the glass to get his attention when I saw a face peep out and **Lost My Nerve**. It had been so long."

"So Hatfield WASN'T the only one in Muckle with a hood," said Nancy. "It did seem unlikely,

what with all the rain you get here."

"Hatfield?" said Crabbit. "Is he the one with the elbows like coat hangers? I saw him earlier getting the bus out of town. We'll not be seeing him again for a while. Can you believe he actually came round here a couple of weeks ago and asked to move in to Stoop's room? Offered me double the going rate for rent, he did. I told him to clear off. I always knew Stoop would need it again one day."

"So he didn't deal with a terrifying Redcap in the cellar?" said Stoop.

"Is that what he told you?" Crabbit said. "Och, it was only Rochester's budgerigar."

He nodded at a cage on the sideboard. A tiny bird sat inside, preening its feathers.

"Hatfield heard it squawking through the open window one day and tried to convince me it was the classic **Mating Call** of an angry Redcap. It would take more than that to fool the father of a mighty monster hunter."

Stoop beamed widely, and informed Nancy and me that he'd be staying on in Muckle for a few days. He had some **Catching Up** to do.*

"What about you two?" inquired Crabbit. "I have plenty of spare rooms upstairs if you want to stay as well."

"We can't," I said. "We have to be up early for school on Monday."

Stoop's dad didn't understand.

"Haven't you been there before?"

"You're wasting your time, Dad," said Stoop. "I've warned them countless times about the danger of **Too Much Education**, but they still insist on going back every day."

The pair of them hadn't stopped shaking their heads in disbelief when Nancy and I set off shortly afterwards for the journey home.

* As well as lots of cupcakes to devour.

# Home Again

Dad rushed out to greet us as we landed expertly in the garden, eager to hear our news.

I couldn't wait to tell him that Nancy was now an official monster hunter too, and that together we'd managed to stop **THE END OF THE WORLD AS WE KNOW IT**.

You don't do that every day.

"You can bring me up to date while we tuck into a celebratory bowl of black stew," he said. "Thankfully, I managed to scrape most of it off the walls after you left. It's not too bad once you pick out the flakes of paint."

To think we'd turned down thirteen trays of cupcakes for this!

"I am glad the world didn't end," I said to Nancy when we were back in our ordinary clothes and sitting in the garden, eating crisps and drinking orange juice to get rid of the taste of the black stew, and writing up a new entry on Noggles in our matching copies of *Monster Hunting for Beginners*. "But when you think about it, the world never does, does it? Everyone's always getting into a flap about some **Impending Disaster**, but things usually work out for the best. Even those silly Sisters of Perpetual Misery came good eventually."

I stopped.

"Did you hear that?" I exclaimed. "I said their name right at last!"

Nancy didn't answer.

"Are you listening to me, Nancy?"

Nancy wasn't. She was staring into space with a look of **Sudden Revelation**. After a long silence, she turned to me and her nose crinkled.

She wouldn't say what she was thinking about, but I knew. She'd remembered what the smell was in Nun Of The Above's room after the explosion.

I blushed redder than Stoop's nose.

I wanted to say, "You try being locked in a room for hours and hours with only a chamber pot under the bed **In Case Of Emergencies!**"

I wasn't to know it would end up all over the walls when the dynamite exploded.

But I didn't say a word. Some sights and smells are too horrifying even for apprentice monster hunters to remember.

**THE END**